BOY
WHO WATCHES

MICHAEL NALIBORSKI

PREFACE

"See it there, just there; follow that crack down to where it forms an oval place like an alcove or a cave. See how it looks like it's been walled in with blocks of stone and maybe a little mud as well," said my river friend as we sat staring across the river at the rock wall on the opposite bank.

"That's not natural," she said. "That had to be done by human hands."

I had been here many times before. Funny, I never really noticed that place in the rock wall before, but it had been there, been there for a very, very long time. It made one think.

We camped there that night. It wasn't far from some Indian cliff-dwelling ruins. We had some people on our trip that wanted to walk over and see them.

One fine supper and more than a few cold beers later, I hit the sack.

That night I dreamed....

Boy Who Watches lay upon the top of the little hill, his body stretched out flat on the hot red earth. A biting fly was in the small of his back, having a very slow and painful lunch, but Boy Who Watches dared not move to kill it. The dreaded Pivanne, the baby eaters, were coming up the river trail!

His hill was more of a little cone-shaped mesa than anything else. There was very hard, very steep rock near the top and a sloping, volcanic talus below. He had climbed the loose talus from the hidden side, so as to hide his steps. The very last steep rock he climbed by using a pole ladder which he pulled up behind him and hid on the flat top of his little hill.

Down below, near the river, the Pivanne came. His father, his mother, Chief Hado, many had warned him that this day might come. That he must always be vigilant, always watching. Boy Who Watches took his responsibility of watching the river trail very seriously, although the older boys of the tribe did not think it to be important work. Chief Hado's own son, Sityatki, took great pleasure in bullying and tormenting him.

Sityatki would rally the older boys to join in ridiculing Boy Who Watches when he left early each morning to keep watch. Now the day had come, the day that the older members of the tribe knew and feared might happen. The Pivanne were coming up the river trail toward the village.

Boy Who Watches slowly peeked to watch the Pivanne come up the river trail. They were not like Boy Who Watches' people— not at all. The one in front seemed to be the leader. He had strange markings on his face, like drawings Boy Who Watches had seen on rock and pottery. He did not look like Boy Who Watches' people, nor did he even look like those he led. The rest of them were staggered very randomly. They did not talk or even look at each other. They did not walk gracefully and quietly as Boy Who Watches' people did. His people would walk closely together even if they were hunting. They would banter good-naturedly between one another when they could. The Pivanne were clumsy and noisy walkers but moved ever forward as if on a mission.

Boy Who Watches knew what their mission was. His heart beat faster with fear as he remembered the stories he had heard many times about the Pivanne. Boy Who Watches knew he must wait, hidden on his little hill, until the Pivanne passed by. He would count the Pivanne. When they were all out of sight, he would signal old Kolichiyaw, who waited on the high mesa beyond.

Boy Who Watches would light the pile of sticks and greenery he had stored on the little hill. Far beyond, old Kolichiyaw waited on the high mesa. He would see the boy's signal smoke and old Kolichiyaw would light his own signal fire. The people of the village would see the smoke from the old man's high mesa. They would gather everything they could from the river valley gardens. They would destroy anything left that could possibly be eaten or used. The people of the village would then climb the slick red rock cliffs, using footholds and the pole ladders they had made. They would take refuge in the Skyhouse far above the river valley. All ladders would be pulled up behind them. The rocks were piled up and ready to be thrown down upon the enemy as they tried to climb the cliffs to Skyhouse. Bow and arrows and throwing sticks were also stockpiled. There the people of the tribe would wait until the enemy left, even if it took months.

It was not always this way. From the stories that his father had told him, Boy Who Watches knew that his tribe had not always lived by the river. Once they had lived far away, near the great peaks. There were other tribes nearby. They planted their squash and beans in the good soil beneath a thin layer of red cinders. There was plenty.

Then a time of little water came. Enemies came from the south and many people died at their hands. Boy Who Watches' ancestors built a house of stone in that place to protect themselves. The house of stone did not work. The older ones retold the stories of the night the entire tribe had to leave that place and run away in the night. Many died at the hands of the Pivanne that night.

Boy Who Watches' people hid far away. It was a bad time. Two of the strongest people sneaked back to look for those missing. To their horror, they found that they had been eaten by the Pivanne.

Those were horrible and hard times, but his people survived. Boy Who Watches' people traveled far, far to the north where a great river flowed. There they found the valley and the cliff with the alcove above where the ones before them had built Skyhouse—a great house of stone, deserted and starting to fall down.

His people repaired and added to Skyhouse. There was water there and they felt safe there. The very young and the very old spent their lives in Skyhouse, never leaving, never going down to the valley and the river below. It was simply too hard to get them up and down the cliff.

Boy Who Watches had fond memories of his childhood in that place. Sunny, carefree, and warm days, playing under the watchful eyes of the old ones of the tribe. Occasionally he looked down into the valley far below. He could see his mother and father there, working in the garden. He remembered his mother standing up to stretch her back and seeing him, looking over the edge far above. She waved at him and he waved back. It filled his heart with happiness then, and now.

There were pleasant, warm memories even in the cold days of winter. Memories of him and his family snug and warm in their small place in Skyhouse. They could hear other families nearby in their own places, talking quietly in the night. Their small fire would warm them there. The air came in from the bottom of the room, through a hole, to feed the fire. All of the smoke would gather and go out the small hole above.

Pleasant memories of that time long ago helped Boy Who Watches lie still and took his mind off the bloodsucking fly in the small of his back. But now that the baby eaters had all finally passed out of sight, he wasted no time in swatting the fly away.

Boy Who Watches jumped up and ran to the back side of the hill where his tinder bundle lay smoldering in a rock crevice. Nervously, he blew into it. Flames erupted from it and quickly he used it to light the pile of dry brush. He gathered the greenery and put it on the fire. The thick smoke rose quickly and silently. Boy Who Watches worried that the Pivanne would somehow see his smoke and come back up the river trail; his gaze shifted from smoke to trail and back again.

Boy Who Watches wanted to wait on his hill until he saw the smoke from the high mesa, which would also be visible from the village and would warn the people of the village of the coming danger. The smoke had to be visible to old Kolichiyaw by now. It was high in the sky and very thick, but he saw no reply smoke from the high mesa. He waited and waited but still no smoke.

Something was wrong. Old Kolichiyaw did not light his fire upon the high mesa. Without the warning smoke from that place, the village would not be warned. His mother, his father, and every one of his tribe might die.

Boy Who Watches waited until he could wait no longer. He decided he must do something. He would run to the high mesa and light the signal fire himself. But it was a long way to the high mesa. He could not make it there before the Pivanne found the village. He had no choice; it was foolish but he must try. Perhaps instead of going a day's journey down the river trail and then back overland to the high mesa on the other side of the river, he could somehow climb the cliffs straight across the river from where he was.

Boy Who Watches lowered the ladder and began running down the talus slope in great galloping hops. He was not careful now to hide his footsteps. He ran straight to the river trail and right across it to the river. He swam across the river and headed directly for the cliffs on the other side. He would have to climb the cliffs first before he reached the mesa and then run to the high mesa beyond. It seemed impossible—he had never climbed these cliffs before, nor did he know if it could be done, but he had to try.

The thick brush on the other side of the river clawed at the boy's skin and made him bleed. The cliff was steep and a climbing route up was hard to find. It was taking a long time, much too long. Then it happened - a slip - dust, and Boy Who Watches was falling through the air. Then darkness and pain!

"O~Hey~OOO~Hey~Hey~OOO," somebody was poking Boy Who Watches and yelling at him. "O~Hey~OOO." Again he felt the stick in his side. It was old Kolichiyaw; he had found him where he lay unconscious. But how, what had happened?

"You are a lucky boy. If it were not for buzzards, I would not know you were here," Kolichiyaw said.

"The Pivanne," Boy Who Watches gasped, "they go toward the village. The people of the village must be warned—you must light the fire."

"Your smoke was seen. My fire was lit and the village surely saw it," Kolichiyaw said.

"But you made no smoke," Boy Who Watches said. "I waited, and I watched for it."

Kolichiyaw hung his head. He looked down between his knees as he squatted down on his haunches. He shook his head and made a "tsk" sound.

"Old Kolichiyaw is not as young as he used to be," the old man said softly. "Kolichiyaw... Kolichiyaw go to sleep and let his fire go out. Kolichiyaw have to make new fire—it take time. But Kolichiyaw make the fire and warn the village." Kolichiyaw's words trailed off as he was still looking down. "I hope village OK."

"You do not know?" Boy Who Watches said as he sat up. He touched his head where there was blood and made a face. "You do not know about the village?" Boy Who Watches said again.

"Old Kolichiyaw did not go to the village," Kolichiyaw said indignantly. "How could I have gone to the village and make it there before the Pivanne?"

"But we must find out! We cannot just stay here," Boy Who Watches said as he stood up and staggered, almost fainting.

"Are you sure, boy?" Kolichiyaw asked. "You don't look so good and it is a long way to go."

"We are going now!" the Boy said sternly and pointed at Kolichiyaw.

Kolichiyaw shrugged as if it did not matter to him. "We are going now."

"How much water did you bring?" Boy Who Watches asked as they started walking.

"Only this one little gourd, and it is almost empty," Kolichiyaw said as he lifted the gourd. "But we could fill it at the river before we go."

"Yes, we can fill it at the river," Boy Who Watches exclaimed and then stopped abruptly. "But we cannot take the river trail. The Pivanne, we would run right into them," he said as if talking to himself.

Boy Who Watches turned and looked at old Kolichiyaw. "How did you get down the cliff to where I fell?" he asked, puzzled. "I could not climb the cliff. How did you?"

Kolichiyaw smiled. "I used the old ones' way," he said smugly. "Kolichiyaw will show you", he said as he started walking, taking the lead now in front of Boy Who Watches. "But first we fill the gourd at the river."

Boy Who Watches followed the old man now, but he was puzzled. How could there be a trail up the cliffs that he did know about? And who were the old ones the old man talked about?

Boy Who Watches knew every path of the river country. He knew every way there was out of the river valley to the high mesa country beyond. And, he knew that there was no trail up these cliffs to the high mesa country for a very long way.

Dutifully though, he followed Kolichiyaw to the river. There they filled the gourd. Without a word, Kolichiyaw turned and started walking back toward the cliffs. Boy Who Watches hesitated, still puzzled, and then followed.

Kolichiyaw walked downriver for a way. It was not easy walking. They clawed their way through thick brush scrambled over loose rock and even had to get in the river a couple of times. They finally came to a thick bramble thicket near a cliff where the old man stopped to look. Boy Who Watches looked at him smugly with his arms crossed. The Boy had been by this place many times, even if it was on the other side of the river, and he knew that there was no trail up the cliffs there or anywhere else near there.

The old man took a few slow steps while he stared at the thicket and then stopped. He bent over at the waist, still staring into the thicket. Boy Who Watches started to speak, but before he could,

Kolichiyaw fell to his hands and knees and, belying his age, zipped through a hole in the bramble as fast as a rabbit!

Stunned, Boy Who Watches squatted down and looked into the hole. Old Kolichiyaw said from the darkness, "You coming?"

Cautiously, Boy Who Watches entered the hole and started to crawl. Boy Who Watches could not see too well in the darkness, but he was aware that they had crawled through the bramble and had come to a hole in the cliff wall.

"Stand up as soon as you enter the cliff tunnel," came the old man's voice from the darkness. "There are climbing holes in the wall—they go straight up. Follow me."

The Boy followed. He saw glimpses of light above as he climbed. Before long, they were out and on top of the cliffs.

Old Kolichiyaw squatted on his haunches looking at him as the Boy emerged on top of the mesa. Boy Who Watches looked around, bewildered. How could he not know about this? Why did old Kolichiyaw never say anything? What else did the old man know?

"We have far to go yet," Kolichiyaw said as he started off across the mesa toward Skyhouse, which stood on the opposite side of the river.

It was almost dark when they reached the mesa rim overlooking Skyhouse on the other side of the river. Kolichiyaw held his hand out to caution Boy Who Watches. Slowly they peeked over the edge.

There were fires below Skyhouse in the valley near the river. The ladders to Skyhouse were all pulled up. Boy Who Watches could faintly hear a child crying. It was getting dark and Boy Who Watches could see forms moving around by a big fire pit in the valley. There was a pole over the fire and something was hanging from it. In shock and horror, Boy Who Watches fell back from the rim and covered his eyes. He staggered back a little way and threw up. Kolichiyaw looked at him and then slowly looked back over the rim. His eyes narrowed and then grew wide. The thing hanging from the cooking pole was a human body! The Pivanne were tearing pieces from it and eating it!

Night closed in quickly and mercifully covered most of the ghastly scene below. Boy Who Watches and the old man did not build a fire for fear of being seen, although being seen on that unreachable high place from below offered little danger to the pair.

The night was filled with unearthly screams from the Pivanne far below. Forms could be seen passing in front of the fire, and Boy Who Watches was not able to sleep. Old Kolichiyaw did not have a problem sleeping and his snoring prompted the Boy to waken the old man.

"Why do they scream so? Will they try to climb Skyhouse tonight?" the Boy asked.

The old man rubbed his face and struggled to comprehend the questions through his sleep fog. "They scream and yell so that those in Skyhouse cannot sleep," the old man finally answered with a sigh. "Most of the Pivanne are sleeping so that they will be rested and strong tomorrow."

Boy Who Watches thought about this answer for a little while and then lay down to rest himself.

It was dawn the next day. The awful realization of what happened had settled in on Boy Who Watches and Kolichiyaw. Grimly and silently they took turns looking over the rim.

Their people down below had taken refuge in Skyhouse. At least one person had been killed and eaten. The thought of who it was kept twisting its way into Boy Who Watches' mind and he shook his head to keep the thoughts out. Perhaps it was not one of their people at all; perhaps it was one of the Pivanne, killed by those in Skyhouse.

It was getting light now. Boy Who Watches sat cross-legged, his back to Kolichiyaw who, was still peeking over the rim.

"What do we do now?" the Boy asked, speaking much too loud for the old man's comfort.

"Shhh!" Kolichiyaw held his hand out with one finger to his lips as he turned to Boy Who Watches and grimaced. "They are stirring now; something is happening!" Kolichiyaw announced.

Boy Who Watches looked over the edge with the old man now. Far below, the Pivanne were moving. Several of the Pivanne were carrying poles they had made from the driftwood piles and were moving toward the cliffs below Skyhouse. Boy Who Watches heard rocks crashing down from Skyhouse as his people threw them at the Pivanne below. The Pivanne leaned their makeshift poles against the cliff and attempted to climb. Suddenly, one Pivanne screamed, grasped his head, and fell. It was over as quickly as it began. The Pivanne retreated out of range through the brush. They left their comrade writhing on the ground at the base of the cliff. Many more rocks came down, some hitting the Pivanne on the ground. He was still now.

"He is dead," Kolichiyaw exclaimed with a satisfied smile. Boy Who Watches hung his head and covered his face with his hands.

"They will never leave now—they have plenty of food," Boy Who Watches moaned. "They will stay. Why should they leave? They have food and water. They have more of their kind of food in Skyhouse. If they can, they will kill and eat all our people," Boy Who Watches said, matter-of-factly.

"What are we to do?" Kolichiyaw said with a shrug.

"We must think, but first we must eat," said the Boy.

Boy Who Watches started walking off away from the rim. Kolichiyaw stared at him for a moment, expressionless, and then silently followed. Away from the canyon rim, Boy Who Watches' mood improved. It felt good to do something so familiar and comfortable, looking for the edible roots and plants that he had always gathered to supplement the squash and beans his people grew by the river, all the while keeping an eye out for the occasional rabbit that thought it could lie still and avoid his sharp eye and sharper arrow or stick. He thought of his precious bow and arrows he had left in Skyhouse. How he wished he had taken them with him when he went to the little hill to be on watch. Perhaps he could use them to kill the Pivanne if he had them. But he knew that would not work— they were many and he was only one. Kolichiyaw was old and useless in that kind of fight.

Far away from the canyon rim, the Boy and old Kolichiyaw found a place to spend the approaching night. They were safe there to build a fire and roast some of the plants they had gathered. Boy Who Watches and Kolichiyaw sat cross-legged near the little fire they had built under a juniper tree, silently eating their meager meal. "Rabbit would be better," Kolichiyaw said. Boy Who Watches did not answer. He stared straight at Kolichiyaw while he slowly chewed a root.

"I am hungry, and these weeds will not fill me," Kolichiyaw complained. "Maybe tomorrow I will build a funnel trap and we will use the fire to drive the rabbits to it," the old man exclaimed cheerfully. Boy Who Watches turned his head slightly to look at Kolichiyaw. He knew that what Kolichiyaw said was only an old man's wishful thinking. It was the conversation made from hunger. Still, it made Boy Who Watches think of happier times.

Boy Who Watches thought back to the hunt he and his father had participated in not so long ago. The men of the village had built a funnel made of sticks at one end of a small valley on the mesa; at the other end of the valley, the brush was set on fire. Men and boys lined both sides of the little valley. They made much noise as they walked just ahead of the fire below them. The rabbits and other rodents fled from the fire and noise and were funneled into a small area made from sticks forming a fence. There, men waited with sticks to club them with. It was much work, but the meat was appreciated by all. The hunt was looked forward to and eagerly anticipated, especially by the boys of the village.

Suddenly, a thought occurred to Boy Who Watches. Slowly the thought took shape and formed in his mind as he closed his eyes to sleep.

The next morning, Boy Who Watches was already awake and staring at Kolichiyaw as the old man awoke. Kolichiyaw stretched slowly on the ground and moaned as he felt all of his years. "Not used to sleeping on the ground," Kolichiyaw said. "Miss my mat."

"I have been thinking… been thinking most of the night. I know how to defeat the Pivanne," Boy Who Watches said.

"Defeat them?" cried Kolichiyaw. "Defeat them! You and me!"

"Yes, you and me," Boy Who Watches said calmly. Boy Who Watches was self-assured. It was strange but he had never felt so certain about something in his life. He knew exactly what he must do. There was no alternative; there was no one else to do it, no one else to help, no one, just he and Kolichiyaw. They must do this thing or die trying. If they did not, there was nothing, no tribe and no future.

Boy Who Watches stood, picked up his stick, and started walking in the direction of Skyhouse. Kolichiyaw watched him, not understanding. Grudgingly, Kolichiyaw simply started following Boy Who Watches.

"This is too much on an old man," Kolichiyaw complained. "We have not even eaten."

Boy Who Watches said nothing, nor did he look back at Kolichiyaw. He dared not talk lest he give rise to his own self-doubt. He had a plan and he knew he must try, but the outcome was anything but certain. He must be brave and not allow fear to creep into him. He was numb as he walked and he felt strangely separated from himself. He was not the same person that he was—he was no longer Boy Who Watches. He must go beyond who he was and become who he would be.

"Awamut, what will we do when we get there?" Kolichiyaw asked sarcastically. "What is your big plan?"

Boy Who Watches abruptly stopped walking and turned to face the old man. The tribe had not called him Awamut (the name he was given at birth) for a very long time. The old man knew this but continued to call him by his birth name.

"I am not Awamut anymore!" the Boy said angrily, even though he hated the new name the tribe had given him—'Boy Who Watches.' Every time he heard it, he thought of the taunts of Sityatki and the other older boys of the tribe. "I am not Boy Who Watches any longer either," he said, more calmly and reflectively. "Do not call me either name ever again." The Boy then turned and continued walking toward Skyhouse.

Kolichiyaw stared at him, bewildered. "Is this boy crazy?" Kolichiyaw mouthed to himself, barely audible. "I must be crazy to follow," he whispered. "But then, what else is there? Just a hungry old man and a crazy boy with no name on a mesa, in the hot sun, walking to their deaths," Kolichiyaw grumbled to himself.

Kolichiyaw slowly started breaking out into a gap-toothed grin. "Hey! I am not Kolichiyaw, the old man who lives on the mesa. I am 'Killer of Our Enemy' and I am coming with 'No Name'! To kill the Pivanne!" The old man stopped walking, pounded one fist to his chest, and looked at the boy.

Boy Who Watches stopped and looked back at him. "So be it", the Boy said. "You are 'Killer of Our Enemy' and I… I am 'No Name'. But you must be quiet now, Killer of Our Enemy, or we will be heard a half day before we get there," No Name said. If it made him be quiet for a while, the Boy would call the old man by whatever name he wanted, at least to his face. But in his mind, the old man would always be Kolichiyaw, the useless old man.

It was almost dark when they arrived at the rim of Skyhouse canyon. They peeked over the edge and looked across the river, where the Pivanne were camped below Skyhouse.

"What now?" Kolichiyaw asked.

"We wait," No Name replied.

For six days they waited, watching the Pivanne. Almost every day the Pivanne went forth and attacked the base of Skyhouse, attempting to climb up to the first ledge, but their hearts were not in it. They were too well fed.

No Name could see the grisly remains of their meals hanging from the pole above the cooking fire. He could see that it was fast disappearing and soon would be gone, which meant that the Pivanne would soon attack Skyhouse with a purposeful vengeance. During each of the Pivanne's attacks, No Name noticed that they were careful not to get hit by the rocks thrown from above. During those days, the Pivanne were busy turning their climbing poles into ladders. They were also making wooden shields, No Name figured, for the purpose of warding off rocks and arrows.

Every day, the Pivanne were more determined in their efforts. No Name knew that it was only a question of time before the Pivanne were able to reach Skyhouse and accomplish their mission of death and destruction.

No Name sat close to Kolichiyaw and spoke to him as the old man was getting comfortable for yet another fireless and hungry night.

"Old man, in the morning I will go downriver, on the rim. I will use the tunnel that you revealed to me. I will cross the river and go up the river trail to where the Pivanne are. I will hide and wait for them to make their attack on Skyhouse. When they do, I will use fire from their pit to set the brush on fire and drive them closer to the base of Skyhouse. There they will burn or be killed by the rocks from Skyhouse. You will stay here."

"Stay here? Stay here! Stay here and do what, starve?" the old man said, a bit too loud for No Name's comfort. "Yesterday I had to eat grasshoppers!" Kolichiyaw whined.

"You will stay here and watch," No Name said. "You are too old and slow to help."

"I am Killer of Our Enemy and you are No Name! Together we will defeat the enemy! I am not Kolichiyaw, the useless old man, who stays here to watch!" Kolichiyaw said angrily.

"You will stay," No Name said again firmly.

Kolichiyaw said nothing more but continued to angrily stare at the Boy and mumble to himself.

No Name lay down to rest in his usual sleeping place, behind the canyon rim. With one hand under his head, he stared blankly at the growing darkness and tried to sleep but could not. He thought of the things he must do in the morning and he was scared. He thought of Kolichiyaw and how the old man wanted to fight the Pivanne, how the old man showed no fear at all.

No Name realized that the old man must know many things that he did not. He thought of how little he really knew of the old man known as Kolichiyaw. How little anyone in the tribe really knew of the old man or his past. He was simply Kolichiyaw, the useless smelly old man who spent his life upon the high mesa, keeping his small fire burning at night and the embers by day, ready to light the signal fire to alert the tribe.

No Name knew that the old man had first encountered the tribe many years ago when the tribe had first discovered the river valley and Skyhouse, or what was left of it from when those before had lived there.

The tribe found Kolichiyaw to be very strange. He spoke of many things that made no sense to the tribe. But, he was not Pivanne, and he spoke the language, for the most part. So the tribe tolerated him and soon they found a way to use him and to remove him from their midst at the same time. So it was that the strange man known as Kolichiyaw was exiled to the high mesa, to live his life watching for a smoke signal.

No Name thought of when he was younger and still known as Awamut. He would travel to the high mesa with his father to take food and to gather stick bundles for the old man. He remembered how he hated the journey, as they would always spend at least one night with the old man in his small stick-and-mud hut before starting the journey back to the tribe. He remembered sleeping with his head outside the door of the hut to avoid the stench of the old man. He remembered Sityatki, who ridiculed him and tormented him when he was given the task of watching the river trail. It was Sityatki who sarcastically gave him the name of Boy Who Watches. How he hated it when the whole tribe started calling him by this name, not knowing how it hurt him.

Sityatki and his cohorts tormented him every chance they got. No Name remembered Sityatki laughing and taunting as he pushed No Name down in front of Moonflower, the girl with the beautiful round eyes who entranced No Name.

As No Name lay in the dust and looked up at Sityatki that day, he heard the older boys' hurtful and stabbing words, that he would take old Kolichiyaw's place on the high mesa someday and the tribe would be rid of him too.

No Name rolled over to his other side and sighed. He must try to sleep before the day came. He must stop thinking of Sityatki and his followers and the old man, Kolichiyaw, the crazy, useless, and stinking old man.

It was not yet dawn when No Name got up. It was just light enough to walk and No Name knew he must go now. He paused to look at old Kolichiyaw, sleeping like a baby. It made No Name sad and lonely. Perhaps he would never talk to anyone of his tribe again. Perhaps the Pivanne would kill him. Perhaps he would become their dinner. Slowly and quietly, No Name walked away.

The way downriver atop the rim was not easy, especially in the pre-dawn light. No Name hurried as best he could, for he knew he must. He felt detached from himself, maybe because of fear or loneliness. He actually wanted to be Boy Who Watches again. But those days were gone and he felt they would never return.

The sun had been up for three hands when he reached Kolichiyaw's tunnel. He found the hand and footholds in the dark and began to descend. He was going too fast and almost fell. There in the dark, he paused and remembered his purpose. It would do no good if he lay dead or hurt at the bottom of Kolichiyaw's tunnel. He descended now more slowly and surely to the bottom. He swam across the river and began walking the river trail that led to the village. He walked as quickly as he could. Long ago, he had learned to jog slowly over great distances, but for now he would walk, perhaps because of the danger ahead or perhaps because he needed to calm his racing heart.

No Name was most of the way to the village when he began to see the smoke. The sun was full on him now and he paused to shade his eyes as he looked toward the village. Sweat ran down his face as he looked, perplexed, at the growing white smoke, the kind of smoke that green brush makes.

Throwing caution to the wind, No Name ran toward Skyhouse. Suddenly, there was a great tearing of bushes on the trail ahead of him. A Pivanne burst from the trail right in front of No Name. He was the one with drawings on his face. The one that No Name had believed was the leader of the Pivanne. He was wild eyed and exhausted; his hair was burnt on one side of his head and was still smoking. His mouth was agape, revealing teeth which were all pointed like those of a wolfdog. Spit drooled down the Pivanne's chin as he stood gasping for air and looking at No Name.

The Pivanne screamed like a wounded animal and rushed toward No Name, grabbing him and throwing him from the trail like a doll. Bewildered, No Name spit the dirt and leaves from his mouth and rolled up to watch the Pivanne running like a deer down the trail, away from Skyhouse. No Name had lost all fear now. He jumped up and began running again toward Skyhouse. In the distance he could hear screaming now, the most awful screaming he had ever heard.

When he drew close to Skyhouse, the awful stench of burning human flesh filled the air. It made No Name nauseated and twice he had to pause, gagging and spitting. He was within sight of Skyhouse now. No Name's fear of the Pivanne was overcome by the surreal scene in front of him.

At the base of Skyhouse, the thick white smoke of burning green bushes billowed up into the air. From the thick of it, an unearthly screaming and wailing emerged. No Name could see rocks being flung from Skyhouse, piercing the smoke below, mercifully putting an end to what was apparently left of the Pivanne. Around the base of Skyhouse and all the way to the river, the vegetation was black and burned or still burning. As No Name's incredulous gaze took in the scene, a movement on the river bank caught his attention—it was Kolichiyaw!

No Name ran to where Kolichiyaw lay. He held old Kolichiyaw's head up and placed it on his leg. No Name's eyes surveyed the sprawled body of the old man, looking for wounds, but there were none. Kolichiyaw's eyes opened and he looked up at No Name.

"We have done it, No Name! We have saved our people!" Kolichiyaw choked as he grasped his chest.

No Name knew the old man was dying. Somehow, the old man had found another way down the cliffs, crossed the river, and carried out the exact plan that No Name had described to the old man.

"Shhh… quiet, Kolichiyaw. Do not try to talk now," No Name said quietly as he wiped the soot from the old man's eyes. The old man reached up and grabbed No Name's arm.

"I am Killer of Our Enemy! I am not Kolichiyaw!" the old man croaked.

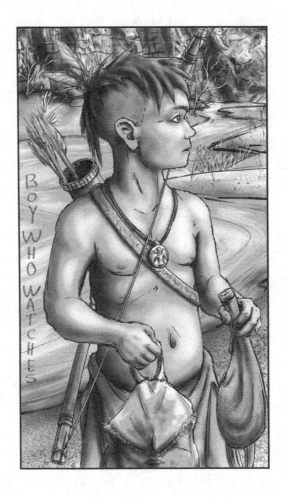

"Yes, you are truly Killer of Our Enemy," No Name said through tears. He had never even wanted to be near the old man before, and now he cried for him. There in the dirt and the soot, the old man shut his eyes and died as No Name held his head and cried.

No Name was still holding Kolichiyaw when he was hit from behind in the head. Stunned and lying facedown in the dirt, he struggled to regain his senses, all the while hearing a familiar voice above him.

"Did you finally decide to come out of hiding, you coward?" the voice said.

No Name rolled over and tried to focus his vision on the person standing above him. He lifted his head and shaded his eyes to see his attacker more clearly. It was Sityatki! Sityatki, his boyhood nemesis, with his group of cronies behind him!

"Get up, coward!" Sityatki hissed.

No Name slowly stood up, brushed himself off, and turned to face his tormentors once again. Somehow, he knew this would not be the same as it had been when they were boys, for No Name felt as though he had grown to manhood in the short time since he had last seen Sityatki. It seemed that Sityatki had also changed. There was something different and more menacing about him.

"Sityatki! I might have known it was you who hit me when my back was turned!" No Name said.

"Chief Sityatki now, coward! Chief Hado is dead!" Sityatki yelled. "I am Chief now and I have seen your cowardice. While brave old Kolichiyaw was saving the village, you were hiding in the bushes!" Sityatki's followers murmured their agreement.

"And now, as Chief, I say you must leave! Leave and never come back!" Sityatki decreed as he stepped forward and pointed to the river trail.

Sityatki's men joined their leader with their bows and arrows pointed at No Name. No Name wanted to tell them the truth. Others of his tribe were not far away now, watching and listening. He could see Moonflower there among them, looking at him sadly. No Name wanted to tell all of them how it was his plan to kill the Pivanne. His plan was to wait until the Pivanne attacked the base of Skyhouse and then set fire to all the brush surrounding them, knowing that the prevailing winds would drive the fire and the Pivanne right to the base of Skyhouse where there would be no escape. He wanted to tell them that, except for an old man's pride, it would have been him that saved the tribe, not Kolichiyaw. But when he opened his mouth to say this, his tormentors only pressed him harder to leave.

"I will tell you one last time, coward! Leave! Leave now! Or I will give the order to kill you!" Sityatki growled as the others drew their bows.

No Name's eyes searched for his father and mother among the onlookers, but he did not see them. No Name had no choice but to turn and go. No Name heard Sityatki yell at him as he walked, looking straight ahead, stiffly down the trail.

"If you come back, we will kill you!"

No Name did not look back. He kept walking until he was far down the trail, away from Skyhouse. He did not know where to go or what to do, except keep walking.

"Awamut, wait!" someone yelled from the trail behind No Name.

No Name stepped off the trail and watched from behind a bush to see who it was that called out his birth name.

"Awamut! Awamut, my son!" yelled No Name's father as he ran up the trail to where No Name was.

No Name and his father embraced each other. It was something they had not done in a very long time. It was not their way to do so.

"Awamut, my son, I had to see you and talk to you. I have brought your bow and arrows, food, and your pack to carry," No Name's father said.

"Father, I cannot leave you and Mother. What am I to do?" No Name asked pleadingly.

"I cannot see any other way, my son. Chief Hado is dead at the hands of the Pivanne. Sityatki and his friends have taken control of the tribe. It is a dark time for the tribe, but I must stay and take care of Mother. We cannot make the journey with you," No Name's father said.

"What journey, my father?" No Name asked, puzzled.

"You must travel toward the setting sun, always toward the setting sun, until you see the big river. A river so big you cannot see the other side of it; it is a walk of many moons. You must go past the high mesa country, past the long pole country, past all that you and I have ever seen. I remember the stories about the big river. Those that live there are of the people; they will stand with you against enemies and they will help you."

"But, Father, the Pivanne will come again against the village. I saw their leader escape," No Name told his father.

"I believe that the Pivanne will never stop coming," No Name's father said as he hung his head. "That is why you must find a new path and live."

"How do you know of this place you talk of, Father? Why must I go there? Why can't I just camp on the high mesa?" No Name pleaded. "You and Mother could join me there. We could make a hut there and hunt and—"

"We cannot, and you cannot," No Name's father interrupted. "The Pivanne will never stop coming. I will speak to the others when I can. I will tell them the truth of things. We must all leave or face the Pivanne again. I fear, son, that they will not listen to me, but you, son, must live. In that your mother and I will take comfort. No matter what happens, son, remember that you are loved. Live, son. Live for us all."

"Father," No Name said with tears in his eyes, "it was my plan to defeat the Pivanne, my plan, not old Kolichiyaw's. I am not a coward."

"Quiet, my son," his father said softly. "There is no need. I know the truth. Take my hand, son, and remember us always as we will remember you. Take this amulet, son, it is like the one I wear. Wear it always as a symbol of our bond."

No Name's father gave him the amulet. It was a hunting talisman of a small eagle carved from sandstone, just like the one he wore around his own neck. No Name took the amulet from his father and placed it around his neck.

"You will have need of these also," No Name's father said as he handed him his bow and arrows, a water skin, and a pack. With this, No Name's father gave one last look at his son, touched his own heart, and then turned and walked back toward Skyhouse.

No Name said nothing more. He fell to his knees and watched his father walk away and disappear down the trail. No Name was alone.

The next morning, No Name awoke, still lying on the trail. He stood up, shook the dust from his hair, and after one lingering look up the trail toward the village, he turned and started his journey, just as his father had advised.

Many lonely days and nights followed. He crossed all the high mesas and wintered near the long pole country where he almost froze to death. Springtime sun shined down on a traveler who did not at all resemble the youth once known as Boy Who Watches. He had grown—he was lean and muscular now. His hair hung down to his mid-back. He was adorned with furs from the animals he had harvested along the way. He had become expert with bow and arrow, snare, and trap. It was only springtime and already he was very dark from the sun. He was ruggedly accustomed to his new life. One could say it even nurtured him.

Far past the long pole country, he entered a country unseen by anyone still living in his tribe. Somehow, he knew, from the stories he had heard as a boy, that it was the land of his grandfather's youth. It was the land they had fled so many seasons ago. It was the land where his people had first encountered the Pivanne.

Strange, broken-down, and abandoned stone houses and fortresses haunted No Name as he explored each one he came to. Here and there, human bones still lay exposed to the sun and wind. In one ruin, No Name was taken aback by a ghastly grinning skull on a ledge within inches of his face as he rounded a corner.

No Name would not spend the nights in the ruins, even though some of them still offered some protection from the elements, there was something unsettling about them. The spirits there seemed to whisper to him of lives that were before, of lives ended too short, and of generations never born, never mourned, never avenged, and never prayed for. Whispered of paths that ended and waited for those who lived to whisper to. No Name did not understand the whispers and could not listen to them when they came to him in the sleep world, so he did not sleep there. He wondered if the Pivanne ever came here again to this dead place, although certainly there was nothing here to offer them anymore.

No Name longed for human contact. Even an encounter with the dreaded Pivanne would not have been unwelcome at this point.

It would not be a mere boy that fought them if they ever met again, No Name mused.

And finally, No Name moved on from that place of death, that place of his ancestors long past. For days, he walked, ever toward the setting sun until one day, he sensed that something amazing lay just ahead. The trees opened up to a great empty expanse from which the clouds seemed to emerge from the earth. No Name reasoned that this must be the birthplace of clouds.

As he drew closer, he realized that it was a great chasm cut into the earth. Never before had he seen anything like this! Never before had he ever heard of anything like this, not even in the campfire stories of the elders. Cautiously, he peeked over the edge and saw, far, far below, a river much like the river valley of his people, but far, far deeper and wider. Was *this* the great river that his father spoke of? But he could easily see the other side of it down below. This river could not be much wider than his own river back home, the home he had no more.

How could he cross this great hole in the earth in order to continue his journey? If it was like the river valley of his youth, he could but walk far enough in either direction and eventually he would come to a place where the canyon flattened out and he could cross. Perhaps this great valley may never end. Perhaps he could find a way down into the great valley and out the other side.

No Name walked for several miles along the rim, finding good access at several points to look again into its depths, but no way to descend appeared possible to him. It seemed hopeless. Night fell and No Name made camp on the rim of the great chasm.

No Name spent the moonlit night with little sleep. Eerie sounds, as if from a demon singing far away, came drifting low and softly upon the wind from the canyon. Twice No Name went to the edge of the canyon to peer into the depths, only to be witness to its foreboding darkness.

The next morning as No Name was getting ready to break camp, he heard that eerie demonic sound again. This time there was no doubt about it; it was real and it was no dream and it was coming from the canyon below. Quickly, No Name rushed to the edge, dropped to his belly, and stared into the canyon. There, far, far below, he could make out figures, three of them walking in line as if on a trail. The lead figure was dressed very colorfully and was wearing a kind of headdress which made him appear even taller than he was. His pack was worn high on his back and beneath his clothing. He had a stick-like object, which he brought up to his mouth whenever he paused. No Name figured that this object was making the strange sounds that he had been hearing. Behind the tall leader came a woman carrying a large basket balanced upon her head. Last followed a very short and stocky figure that walked very stiffly and awkwardly. He carried nothing but a small pack and a stick to steady him.

No Name lay upon his belly for a long time watching their progress up out of the canyon. He could now make out the crude trail they followed and his eyes traced its apparent route up to the rim. No Name decided to make his way to that place and be there waiting when the trio emerged from the canyon.

No Name's instinct told him to go the other way, to avoid these strange people. But an overwhelming yearning for human contact, and the fact that these people probably knew a way past this canyon, compelled him back to the rim. He would be ready to stand and move out quickly to intercept the trio at the place on the rim where he expected them to emerge. No Name arrived at that location just before they climbed out of canyon. He awaited them, bow and arrow at the ready, prepared to fight them or to kill them if necessary but not before he found out who or what they were. If they were Pivanne, he would surely kill them. If they were demons, they might enchant him and enslave him. Now they were close, so close he could hear one of them singing. Amazingly, he could make out the words of his own language!

"I am Locust

I am Locust

I bring seeds

I bring salt

I bring honey

And blessed cornmeal

All for you"

No Name stood, at the ready, in plain sight of the trailhead as they emerged. All three of them stood on top of the rim now, pausing to rest after their arduous walk. They were apparently oblivious to No Name standing just a stone's toss away with arrow drawn back and pointed straight at them.

No Name's heart leapt as he viewed the tall one in front. He was very tall, even taller that No Name himself. He wore a headdress with strange long feathers and a colorful blanket with holes for his head and arms that covered his entire body. Between the tall one's shoulder blades and high on his back was a large bulbous hump under the blanket. What No Name had originally thought was a pack was not a pack at all, but rather a strange growth.

The woman with them sat her large basket down. She was plain looking and not very unusual, except for the way she wore her hair in tight large rolls on the top and sides of her head.

No Name shifted his gaze to the small one in the back of the group. He audibly gasped as he viewed the monstrosity in front of him. The three heard him and all three froze as they now stared back at No Name. No Name walked forward as his gaze and aim shifted nervously from one person to another. His eyes grew wide as he again focused his attention on the small one.

The small one was hideously deformed with only one arm visible and legs of uneven length. He was shorter than most children but wide with a bulging barrel chest much bigger than a normal man's chest. The small one grimaced as he stared back at No Name, revealing horrible jagged and rotten teeth.

The tall one held out his hand as if to stop the other two from doing anything. "Are you here to gather the salt, young person?" said the tall one calmly.

"What is salt?" No Name heard himself ask. "And how is it that you speak my language?"

"I speak your language because that is what I speak," the tall one said. "I knew when I saw you that we are of the same people, separated by different clans with different paths in this world. And as for salt, it is salt; it is as a mother to the child, as sun to the earth, as rain to the corn. How is it that you do not know salt? It is sacred and in this canyon is where you must go to gather it."

No Name cocked his head and squinted his eyes inquisitively but did not relax his drawn bow.

"Please put down your bow, we mean you no harm," the tall one said. "Put it down and I will show you salt. You may hold it and taste it. I will show you and tell you many things which you, my brother, do not know."

Slowly, No Name relaxed his pull and lowered his weapon. The tall one looked around, found a good rock, exhaled heavily, and sat down. He took off his headdress and then removed his cloak, revealing a hump high on his back between his shoulders. As he placed the cloak on the ground, be noticed No Name's hard stare at his back.

"A deformity since birth, much like the small one, except my people kept me and even revered me. His people were going to throw him off a cliff before I intervened," the tall one said as the small one grinned widely toward No Name.

"We will camp here. I am tired," the tall one said loudly to the other two.

They quit looking at No Name and immediately started making camp on the rim of the great canyon.

"All peoples come to know me as 'Locust,'" the tall one announced. "The woman I call 'Helper' and my little friend is 'Toad.' What do they call you?" Locust asked.

"I call myself 'No Name.' My people know me no longer. They have driven me from them—thrown me away, much like your little friend, Toad."

"Ah! Another reject! You are welcome, No Name," said Locust. "Camp with us. I have much to tell you and to show you, the first of which is salt!"

Locust stood up and walked over to where Helper had sat her great basket. He came back with a small leather pouch from which he poured a small amount of contents into his hand and extended it to No Name. No Name slowly took a pinch of it and looked at Locust inquisitively. Locust motioned to his own mouth, instructing No Name to taste it. No Name placed the pinch in his mouth and promptly spit it out, making an awful face.

"Ha!" Locust laughed. "It is only good on food. Cook enough for another tonight," he yelled to Toad.

Toad came closer to No Name and questioned him intently. "Do you prefer your meat on a stick or in a pot?" he asked, cocking his head to one side.

It was the first time No Name had heard Toad speak. He hesitated as he was transfixed by the strange little voice in front of him, but finally he answered: "It has been a long time, but I prefer my food cooked in a pot."

"A pot! A pot!" Toad hollered excitedly as he leapt around, celebrating as he awkwardly flailed about.

No Name was taken aback by this unexpected outburst and looked at Locust for some sort of explanation.

Locust saw No Name's concern, shrugged, and answered the unspoken question: "Toad is happy that you are of the people and not of the 'Headbangers.' You see, he still had doubt but he knows that a Headbanger would never eat his meat cooked in a pot. You may sleep soundly tonight; it would have been very dangerous if Toad thought you were a Headbanger."

No Name figured that they were talking about the Pivanne but did not question them about it. That night he ate the best meat he had ever tasted. Truly this 'salt' was all Locust said it was. No Name felt that there was much to learn from these new friends. For tonight, though, No Name found a good place to sleep, far enough back from the fire to allow him to keep an eye on his newfound friends.

No Name awakened abruptly in the morning by the same demonic sounds that he had heard emanating from the trio in the canyon on the previous day. In his half-awake and half-asleep state, he lurched clumsily to his feet and staggered about looking for his bow.

Locust stopped playing, put down the flute, and looked at No Name with amazement. "It is a flute! A flute, my brother. Please tell me that your clan remembers what a flute is," Locust asked incredulously.

No Name had not found his weapon yet, so he pointed his finger at Locust. "Put down the demon stick! If you are a man and not a demon, then put it down!" No Name demanded.

"It is a flute. It makes music and it has been known to my clan since this world began," Locust said assuredly. "Let me play it and you will see that it is good, not bad."

Slowly, cautiously, Locust put the flute to his lips and began to play.

No Name was frightened but did not run. He looked at Helper and Toad, who were simply sitting and listening contentedly to the strange sounds. Soon he found himself sitting and listening, hypnotized by the strange, beautiful new sounds.

"Never be afraid of the things that men make. Take them to yourself and master them," Locust said as he stopped playing and handed the flute to No Name.

No Name took the flute and looked at it in his hands, not knowing what to do with it.

"Blow into it, blow into the end of it," Locust urged.

No Name looked at Locust with his mouth agape and slowly moved the flute end to his mouth. Suddenly, Toad burst into a shrill shriek of a laugh and grinning hideously, pointed at No Name with his one hand. No Name glared at Toad and, realizing what Toad was laughing at, switched the flute around and quickly blew into the correct end of it.

Tweeeee! Came the shrill, untrained, and clumsy sound from the flute. No Name jerked it from his lips and laughed out loud with glee as he looked, amazed, at the instrument in his hand.

"Ha ha ha ha ha ha!" he was joined in a bout of laughter by Locust and Toad as Helper sat grinning.

"By the time the days grow cold, you will be an expert on the flute!" Locust declared. Locust spoke to him as if it were understood that he would travel with the trio. Although No Name had already been thinking about that possibility, he could not get his father's advice out of his head.

"Surely you have much to teach and I much to learn from you," No Name said somberly. "But I must go to the big river that lies toward the setting sun. A river so big that you cannot see across it.

There, the people are great and many and they will help me. This my father has told me."

Toad started to laugh again but was silenced by Locust's outstretched hand. "How did your father know of this 'big river' and the people of the big river?" Locust asked No Name.

"I do not know how he knows but it is beyond anything my father or even his father has ever seen," No Name confided.

Locust stood up and slowly walked back and forth. He was deep in thought and talked softly as he walked. "In fact, your father's words have truth about them. But the truth has been clouded by generations of forgotten stories, rituals, and ceremonies that were never passed on to the young ones. I know that your clan must have suffered for they are lost in the dark and have forgotten the commands of the Creator. They have strayed from their path of life. Their spirit is sick and must be healed."

Locust stopped walking and looked at No Name. Locust had a faraway look in his eyes. "Healed by a castaway son; by one born anew," Locust said in a yet softer voice.

No Name had a puzzled look, and it was apparent that he knew not of what Locust speaks.

"You follow your father's advice and travel to the big river. In order to do so, you must cross this great canyon. Is that not so?" asked Locust.

"It is what I must do," replied No Name.

"Well then, come with us. We travel now to the village of the basket makers who live in this very same great canyon many days' travel from here. If you are still determined, I will show you a place where it is possible to cross the river and climb out of the canyon to continue your journey. But I must warn you, if you decide to cross the river and continue your journey, we must perform a ceremony at that time to ask permission for you to cross the river. This you must do or I cannot show you the way out."

"Why must I ask permission to cross this river and whom do I ask?" asked No Name, perplexed.

"You have strayed from your path of life, but I have not," Locust said. "I am bound by honor to tell you the truth of things. The river is a boundary of the peoples' land. Permission to cross out of the peoples' land must be asked of the Creator. All people who are on the true path of life must indeed leave the center of the universe many times."

No Name was even more confused than before, but considering his choices, decided to give his word to Locust and travel with them to the village of the basket makers. "I give you my word to ask permission before I cross the river and continue my journey. I will do this thing just as you instruct me to," No Name promised.

"It is good," Locust said in approval. "Break camp! We journey today!" he yelled at Helper and Toad.

Helper heaved the large basket back upon her head to start their journey. Toad slung his loaded pack over his head and stump of his missing arm. Locust donned his feathered headdress and picked up his flute to start the journey. No Name slung his own modest pack and bow over his shoulder and began to walk behind Helper, who dutifully fell in behind Locust.

HELPER

No Name felt sorry for Helper and wanted to help carry some of her great burden. "Let me help carry part of your load," No Name said to Helper, getting her attention.

"This is my job. I am Helper," she said matter-of-factly.

No Name was stunned; he had never heard Helper say a word. He assumed she could not, or would not, speak. He looked astonished at Toad in his moment of revelation.

"I am Toad. I cook. I clean," Toad offered in answer.

Locust stopped walking and looked back at his companions. "Ah, yes. Everyone has a job and I can see that we must give you a job as well. I suspect that you are good with that bow and arrow, and so, we will call you 'Protector'! And that will be your job, to protect us with bow and arrow! Believe me, there are many occasions when someone handy and ready with bow and arrow would be useful to us."

After a moment of silence, Helper grunted in approval. Toad grinned and nodded. No Name shrugged and unshouldered his bow to have ready. And so it was decided. The journey continued.

As they walked, No Name considered his new job as protector. He wondered if he should tell Locust that he had never actually killed anyone with bow and arrow, although he had gotten quite good with the weapon since he was driven from the tribe. *Oh, well*, he thought, *if this is what they want.* He only had to be a protector until they parted company after their journey to the basket makers' tribe.

The days passed without event. They stayed close to the rim of the great canyon when they could. Its beauty moved them all, although not one of them spoke of it—they didn't have to. Three out of four days, No Name was able to supply fresh meat for the nightly cooking pot. On the fifth day they camped early near the rim of the canyon and No Name decided to go hunting while the others set up camp and rested.

No Name had good luck and was heading back to camp with a fat rabbit when he was frozen by what he saw happening at camp.

There in the bushes, right behind a resting Locust, a pair of strange men were sneaking up on him. Each had a large rock in hand and their intention appeared to be murder.

No Name did not have much time to act. He could yell a warning easily enough, but by now the pair were close enough to use their rocks and surely a yell might prompt them to do so. Quickly No Name dropped the rabbit and silently moved toward the pair, with arrow strung and ready. His eyes never left the pair as he quickly drew closer and closer. Somehow his feet, trained by countless hunts and stalks, knew where to step missing every tuft of grass and every small twig that could snap and give his approach away.

He was close now, well within arrow range, when the first one raised his large rock over his head with both hands in preparation to throw it down upon Locust's resting head. No Name's arrow was quick and accurate.

The shaft went through the first one's neck, stopping with the arrowhead fully visible, sticking out the other side. It was stained crimson blood red now. The stricken attacker fell to the ground with a horrible gurgling scream. Kicking and screaming, he spent his last moments of life. No Name strung another arrow and looked immediately for the other attacker, but he had dropped his rock and, running through the brush with wild-eyed abandon, was already out of range.

PROTECTOR

By this time, Locust and the others were alerted and began to realize what was happening. They all seemed to gather on cue around the dead man lying on the ground.

"Headbangers!" Locust loudly announced. "They would have surely killed us all were it not for you! As surely as the sun is setting, we owe you our lives," Locust said, looking at Protector with new-found admiration.

Protector said nothing; he felt sick as he looked upon the life-less form lying on the ground in front of him. It was the first time he had ever killed another, although the others did not know this.

"Will the other come back?" Protector asked Locust.

"Most likely not; they are cowards. But they are starving cowards, so we would be wise to keep watch tonight just in case," Locust replied.

Everyone took turns keeping watch that night. Toad cooked the rabbit Protector had brought back to camp. Everyone ate quietly without the usual camp talk. Afterwards, Protector found the opportunity to ask Locust a question that had been bothering him.

"What is the difference between Headbangers and the Pivanne?" Protector asked.

"The world we know is full of peoples," Locust said. "But many of them are not 'of the people.' Not the same as you and I. I believe the Headbangers are animal spirits that have taken human form. I have had a vision and in that vision I saw that Creator made man and gave him a man's spirit. Creator also made the animals and gave them animal spirits. Some of the animal spirits were powerful and they were jealous of man. Some animals were able to take man's form and began to imitate the people. These animals imitated man for so long that they believe they are man and have forgotten their true form. They have lost their spiritual power as animals.

"The Pivanne or man-eaters," Locust continued, "were of the people in a different world. They have transgressed against the Creator and have been cast out, for they eat their own kind. They were of the people, but now they imitate the animals. Someday, they will fully become the animal they imitate. They have lost their spiritual power of the man and will never have the spiritual power of the animal."

Protector fell asleep contemplating what Locust told him.

In the morning, Protector helped Toad drag the Headbanger's body to the rim of the great canyon and throw it over the edge. Locust said it was a fitting burial for that one. Protector spent a few moments quietly looking at the body sprawled out on a rock far below before it was time to travel on.

In the few days it took to reach the basket makers' canyon, which in turn fed into the great canyon, Locust seemed driven to teach Protector as many ceremonies, rituals, beliefs, and stories as he possibly could. Strange thing was that they were starting to make sense to Protector, and he was starting to look forward to them.

They camped but a half-day walk away from the basket makers' village. Locust felt it was time to perform the ceremony asking permission for Protector to cross the river and leave the peoples' land to continue his journey alone.

First, Locust positioned Toad and Helper some distance away from their camp—one up the canyon and one down the canyon—as guards. What they were to guard against, Protector did not know, as each was armed with only a feather and a gourd rattle. Locust made lines of corn meal in all four directions. He then placed feathers in all four directions before building a smoky fire with green spruce. Protector gagged as Locust wafted the thick smoke about and chanted inaudible prayers. Occasionally Locust would cast some powder from a pouch upon the fire, which made the smoke even more acrid and unbearable to Protector's nostrils. Hours passed and

Protector was only required to sit and watch and be irritated by the toxic smoke.

Suddenly the ceremony was apparently over. Locust simply stopped his chanting and smoke making and sat down to rest and quench his thirst with a liquid in a covered pot near the fire. He offered some to Protector, and Protector drank deeply of the soothing liquid.

"Is the ceremony over, has permission been granted?" Protector asked.

"I do not know," said Locust, wiping his brow and removing his headdress.

"How am I to know if I may cross the river?" Protector asked, puzzled.

"You will know," Locust said as he lay down. "You will know."

The whole thing was quite strange. How would he know if he may cross the river or not? And where were Toad and Helper? Why didn't they come back to camp? Protector did not understand and Locust was sleeping now. Protector was too tired to worry about it. *Perhaps Locust would explain it in the morning*, he thought as he drifted off to sleep.

That night Protector dreamed, more vividly and real than real itself. He had experienced vivid dreams before, but this was different. Before, when he had a very vivid and disturbing dream he would wake immediately. There was no startled waking from this dream, if it *was* a dream.

He dreamed that he had awakened to some small noise late in the night. The fire was but a few smoking embers glowing in the moonless night. Protector got up and moved carefully in the dark to kneel by the embers. He paused, listening intently to the dark.

Hearing only the common night noises, he prepared to lie down when he heard it again.

Coming up from the canyon—chanting and singing. Protector listened for a moment and then quickly gathered a few twigs that lay around the fire circle. Blowing and working quickly, he got another small fire going so he could see more clearly. He went over to Locust to shake him awake. There was a form under the sleeping blanket; Protector touched it. It collapsed and fell almost flat. Throwing back the blanket, Protector could see, in the faint light, quickly disappearing multitudes of ants that constituted the form and image of a sleeping Locust. Protector then turned and looked for Helper and Toad, but they were not in camp. Could it be that they had never come back to camp?

Should he stand and fight or should he turn and run? Certainly there was no one here to protect except himself. Protector decided to get his bow and at least find out what was coming up from the canyon. Maybe it was only a delegation from the basket makers' tribe coming to welcome Locust, their old friend. Where was Locust? He would know what to do, if only he was here!

Protector grabbed a large stick that had ignited from the fire and used it as a torch to see those who came. Squinting and holding the torch high, Protector realized that this was not such a good idea; they could see him much better than he could see them.

Abruptly a figure emerged from the dark and stood directly in front of Protector. Protector was startled and took a step back, dropping his torch. Protector did not retreat further for he could clearly see the strange one's legs in the torch light. He could see that the strange one stood there looking at him, not moving.

"Choose! Choose one to have and one to give to the others!" Strange One boomed at Protector.

"Choose what?" Protector asked. "I cannot see."

"Pick up the torch and choose one. One is yours and the other you must give to the others," Strange One answered.

Slowly, Protector reached down and picked up the torch, all the while keeping his eyes up at the darkness where Strange One was surely looking back at him. He lifted the torch to see what the Strange One spoke of. Strange One held two very large round gourds, one in each hand. Of these, he apparently wanted Protector to choose one. When Strange One spoke again, Protector looked at Strange One's face; he loudly gasped at what he saw, but he did not run. Strange One did not have the head of a man! Strange One had the head of an eagle!

"Choose one to keep and one to give to these others!" Strange One loudly announced again.

"What others?" Protector asked.

"THESE OTHERS!" Strange One boomed again, even louder than before. He took the torch from Protector to show him. Strange One held the torch high and Protector could see the others he spoke of as the whole valley became strangely very visible from the light of the torch.

Behind Strange One and across the width of the entire valley floor and as far as Protector could see were the ones Strange One spoke of. Like worms twisting in the dirt lay thousands of dirty, withered, starving human children, mouthing words unheard, begging and pleading.

Strange One moved the torch and his attention back to Protector and Protector could see the horrible sight no more. "You must choose now! Choose the right or choose the left. CHOOSE!" Strange One commanded.

Slowly Protector reached out and touched the gourd on his left with his finger.

"You have chosen wisely," Strange One said and threw the chosen gourd on the ground in front of Protector. The gourd broke in halves and instantly from each half shone brilliant beams of different colored light which lit up the entire valley. Then, from each half, a stalk of corn grew to an amazing height in the blink of an eye. Ears of corn burst forth from their husks, revealing corn of many colors— like the corn seeds that Locust carried to all tribes that he met.

"The light is my promise of knowledge to you," Strange One proclaimed. "The corn is my promise of plenty to you for all your time. You have but to accept these gifts."

"But what of them?" Protector asked, pointing to the multitudes who still thrashed about in the dust behind Strange One, quite visible now in the multicolored light from the gourd.

"They will have... this!" Strange One said loudly and threw the remaining gourd into the midst of the multitudes.

It broke in two, just as the other gourd had done, but no light came forth from it, no corn grew from the pieces. It was only a dry and hollow gourd with only a few rattle beans that fell out upon the ground when it broke. A great wailing and crying could now be heard from the many as their misery grew even worse because of the bleak revelation of the empty gourd.

"Since I have so much, cannot you give them some of what I have?" Protector asked of Strange One.

"I cannot; what has been given is given and is mine no longer," Strange One said.

Protector did not know what to do, but he knew he could not stand much more of this wailing and crying, which was growing louder and louder. Protector reached down, picked up one half of the gourd in front of him, and heaved it at the many with all his strength.

The piece of gourd landed among the many and instantly the din of wailing and crying ceased. The thousands of maggot-like forms upon the ground began to grow fatter and healthier. Their lamentations of misery turned into soothing sounds of contentment.

Then an even more amazing thing happened. Each form upon the ground turned into a bird. Each bird flew up into the canyon air to join in a great swirling, squawking crescendo of flight. The great mass of birds was divided into four groups. Each group flew off in a different direction—East, West, North, South—until they disappeared from sight.

The canyon suddenly grew quiet and the light from the gourd faded away as Protector stood looking up into the canyon sky. Protector looked around for Strange One, but he was gone. Only the ordinary night sounds greeted Protector as he walked back to camp. He looked at Locust, who was sleeping soundly as if nothing had happened. So too were Toad and Helper, in their respective spots, sleeping like babies. How was it that they had not witnessed the wonders which Protector had seen? Protector sat upon his mat contemplating the wonders he had seen on this strange night. He was exhausted. Sleep came again as his head hit his mat.

Morning came too early for Protector. He sat upon his sleeping mat and held his aching head. Locust offered him a bowl of soup with fresh squash and corn from Toad's cooking pot.

"Where did you get this?" Protector asked. He had not had fresh corn or squash since he left the village, and he had never had corn or squash quite like this.

"The basket makers brought it to us this morning. It was grown from the seed I brought to them on my last visit. They know we are here and eagerly awaited our arrival. You were still sleeping like the dead; you did not even hear them. You must have not gotten much rest," Locust said, studying Protector for a reaction.

"Something strange happened to me last night. Did you not see, did you not hear anything, nothing?" Protector asked. "I do not know if it was a dream or if it was real," he said, shaking his head.

"After the ceremony, I went to sleep," Locust said. "I was awakened sometime later by Toad and Helper, who were returning from their stations in the canyon. We built up the fire and sat and talked. You slept. Nothing unusual happened last night, other than the ceremony we performed. What happened to you happened in your dreams, but that does not mean that it was not real. Remember, you did ask Creator for permission to leave the peoples' land and continue your journey. How did you think he would answer you, by walking up the canyon and talking to you?" Locust asked, half smiling.

Protector looked at Locust, stunned and incredulous. How close Locust was to the truth in his jesting. Perhaps Creator did walk up the canyon and talk to him last night. Locust could tell by Protector's reaction that he had struck a nerve with his banter, so he sat down beside Protector and spoke more seriously now.

"Tell me the dream, everything, every detail. Perhaps I can help you make sense of it. The basket makers can wait."

They spent a long time sitting there on Protector's mat, Protector talking, Locust listening. Finally, the story of his night told, Protector sat quietly, looking at Locust. Locust sat still for a few moments, thinking, and then began to speak.

"The ceremony we performed was for permission for you to leave the peoples' land. I believe that your spirit guide came up from the Great Canyon, where all spirit guides dwell, to give you an answer to your request. He did not grant or deny permission to leave; he merely showed you what the future held in either decision. The gourd you chose was a gift from the Creator, a chance to regain what was lost. The stories, the rituals, the ceremonies, and the dances, these were the beams of light that came from the gourd. Just as different colors of sunlight warm each world of our existence, so too are these things necessary for the true peoples' spiritual power. The corn was sustenance, life itself, a promise of nurturing from Mother Earth.

"When you gave these things to the pitiful forms on the canyon floor, you in fact gave these gifts to your descendants, the descendants of your clan for all time. It means that you can teach and give these gifts to your tribe. They in turn will hold and pass them on to the children and the children of the children and the children of all the worlds to come.

"I believe you will return to your tribe at some time, regardless of your decision to leave or stay in the peoples' land. You will return and you will pass these gifts on to them. They will regain their path of life. They will thrive and multiply. From your one clan, four will be born and they will travel to all four directions of this world, just as the birds divided and flew off to all four directions. Someday, all will return to the peoples' land, their final home, and their spirits will have power, having kept the commands of the Creator." Locust caught his breath and then continued.

"Only the true spirit guide came up the canyon. False ones were kept away by Helper and Toad, posted in the canyon as spirit guards. Toad and Helper did not see or hear anything; they merely did as I told them to do, as the ancient rituals dictated, just as I was taught by the old ones of my clan.

"The experience was real enough, for you only. Your spirit left this world and entered the world of the spirits. That is why nothing unusual happened to anyone except you."

"What of the ants who had your form when I threw back your blanket?" asked Protector.

"That is a matter that concerns only me," Locust answered with a distant look in his eyes. "Perhaps someday you will understand its meaning. But for now, break camp! Tonight we dine at the basket makers' camp."

Locust gave Protector much to think about, but for now he was preoccupied with their visit to the basket makers' camp. After a short walk down the canyon, they arrived and were greeted with great fanfare. Locust was treated like a great chief as he was placed on a chair and lifted and carried about the village. Every person was encouraged to join in the joyful and raucous procession.

Protector had never experienced anything like this. Locust's arrival at the basket makers' camp inspired a celebration in his honor. There was much food prepared and served, including fish so large that it had to be hung from a pole by two strong men to be cleaned and cut up. Locust told him that the people raised the large fish in pools nearby and harvested them at will.

Locust played his flute for all and the entire tribe grew quiet as they were entranced by the music. Beautiful young basket maker girls looked at Protector adoringly, stirring strange new feelings in him. One of them looked like Moonflower, the beautiful girl of his own tribe who made his heart race and paralyzed his ability to speak in what seemed like a different lifetime, long ago. She said something to Protector, but he did not understand. Locust told Protector that the girl wanted to know if he would like 'spulka' to drink. Protector motioned that he would and she went to fetch him a bowl of the liquid. Locust told him to be careful, as it would put bees in his head.

The next morning, early, found Protector sitting by the smoldering communal campfire, thoughtfully fingering the sandstone eagle amulet that hung around his neck.

"You are up early this day," Locust says to him as he throws an armful of fresh wood on the campfire. "I was thinking that the bees in your poor head would have stolen your mind away."

"I was careful not to drink too much. I have never known such drink," Protector said, and as if thinking out loud, added, "There is much that I do not know, much I have not seen, much I could learn."

"What does this mean? That you want to learn how to make spulka?" Locust asked Protector, narrowing his eyes.

"Noooo!" moaned Protector, changing the mood. Just as quickly, he changed the mood again, becoming serious and looking directly at Locust. "I have made a decision," Protector announced. "If you will still have me, I would like to continue with you on your journeys. This is my vision, my destiny to travel with you and learn all I can learn. Someday I will return to my people and face what may come. To give back what I have been given. These things I will do and fulfill my vision."

"So you have said and so it will be," Locust said and grasped Protector's arm in brotherhood.

Seven summers passed and once again Protector sat deep in thought, slowly fingering the small stone eagle amulet that hung from his neck. It was a different Protector now, grown to the fullness of manhood. He had seen much, done much, and learned much in his travels with Locust. They had traveled south until they could go no further. They returned along the same route until they now neared the peoples' land where they first met long ago.

They had encountered those of the people whose spiritual power was great and their feet were on the true path of life. They had also met those who had strayed from the path. They had encountered the Pivanne and the Headbangers and sometimes they had to fight them. Protector earned his name many times.

Along the way, in the land of the talking birds, Helper grew too old to continue and stayed with the people of that clan to live out her days. She was quickly replaced by two women of the Matawan tribe. It seemed that there was no shortage of women who would gladly spend their lives traveling with and helping Locust, the great man, a revered legend almost everywhere they went.

In true form, Locust renamed both of the women 'Helper.' This seemed strange and confusing to Protector at first, but he grew to understand and accept that the women were just that, helpers, to Locust. He seemed to have no emotional attachment to them. They were there to 'help' and that was all. Locust's attitude toward the women was reciprocated by adoring looks and glances by the women (when he was not looking), which betrayed their dutiful service. They, just like the original Helper, learned to speak little and do much.

Toad still traveled with them, although he had grown older. These days he seemed to have much more trouble even walking and keeping up with the group. Much of the time he could not even perform his cooking duties, a task gladly taken up by the Helpers.

Protector wondered why Toad even bothered to continue these journeys with Locust. Clearly, he loved The Great Man just as the original Helper surely did. Protector remembered the day that Helper stayed behind with the Matawan people, to live out her winter days in comfort. Locust shed not a tear when it was time to leave, not even bothering to look back and wave goodbye as both Protector and Toad had done. Tears flowed freely from Helper's eyes as she sat and watched them leave. True to what was always expected of her from Locust, she said not a word nor made a sound as he walked out of her life.

Protector's thoughts were interrupted by Locust's hand upon his shoulder.

"What troubles you this day, Protector?" Locust asked. "Is it that we near your homeland, the place of your youth and your mother and father?"

"We are close to those things and more," confirmed Protector. "I return to face my destiny."

"What destiny is that? To face many who would kill you? There is no need. We have bypassed many places in the past, many tribes that offered nothing but trouble. We could bypass this place also," Locust offered.

"I do not expect you to go with me. I must face this alone. When it is time, I will say goodbye," Protector said, trying not to let sentiment taint his voice. He had seen Locust's detached, unemotional goodbyes and doubted that this would be a problem for him.

Locust merely looked at him for a moment, then turned and continued what he was doing. "Tomorrow morning we reach the trail into the Great Canyon that leads to salt, which we will need to collect for trade," Locust announced.

The morning found the group walking down the trail into the Great Canyon. The same trail where Protector had first seen Locust and Toad years before. Locust played his flute as they walked. The canyon seemed to play the music back at them in an eerie, beautiful sort of way. Suddenly a chill came onto Protector; the sound must be heard for miles. Who else was listening just as he had long ago?

"Maybe we should go quietly. The sound is carrying and it appears that many more use this trail than just us," Protector said.

"Those who use this trail are of the people. They are on the true path of life and will not harm us," Locust replied. "When we reach the salt, we must perform one more ceremony that you have not learned yet. It is the last one you will need to know before you reach your home."

"Do not forget that I heard you coming long before I saw you many years ago, as I lay upon the rim of this Great Canyon," Protector said.

"You have a good point," Locust said thoughtfully. "But who is to say that Creator did not mean for your ears to hear us? If we travel each path of life afraid to make music lest someone hear it, then we will arrive at our destination safely but we will have never truly walked our intended path."

Locust put the flute to his lips and began playing again. Protector continued to watch the cliffs warily and thought about these words, not so much about Locust's idea on life and music (these things he had heard before and expected from Locust) but rather what Locust told Protector about the ceremony he must learn before 'he' and not 'they' reached Protector's old home. It was what

Protector expected, although sadly, he did not look forward to parting company and yet he knew this day must come.

The journey to the salt went without trouble, even though Locust played his flute loudly all the way. The salt ceremony was performed and was learned. The salt was gathered and loaded into the baskets for future trade. The walk out of the Great Canyon was both beautiful and dangerous, as Locust insisted that they travel by moonlight, true to form, playing his flute all the way out.

On the rim again, they took a final look at the Great Canyon before heading away from it. "We travel toward a different river valley now—your river valley, I believe," Locust said to Protector. "But that river valley offers no trade. I have never traveled its length, but instead we must travel on to another great river to the north and traverse its length, trading with many friendly tribes there. This we must do before the snow falls, for there is a hut and stores waiting for us, for we will not survive that high place without shelter."

"Then I must say goodbye at my river valley and hope that the Creator will watch over your journey and see you safely to your warm winter hut," Protector said without emotion.

Locust looked at him silently for a few moments, neither confirming nor denying this scenario as eavesdropping Toad stared at both of them, frozen, with his mouth open.

They made good time and in a few days they came to the place of Protector's grandfather's youth, now even more forlorn and dead than Protector remembered.

"Nothing lives here," Locust said. "Perhaps we should shelter here for the coming night."

"I know this place of death," Protector said. "Sleep here? I cannot. There are voices here that try to talk to me."

Locust looked at him with an understanding stare, but before he could answer, the moment was broken by Toad's raucous laughter.

"EE-yah! EE-yah!" Toad bellowed as he hoisted skyward a grinning skull mounted on a long pole. "EE-yah! EE-yah! He will lead our way!" Toad screamed with glee.

Angrily, Protector got up and rushed toward Toad. He jerked the pole from him and the skull fell into the red dust. Protector drew back his arm as if to strike Toad, but instead dropped to his knees and covered his eyes and sobs.

"There are voices here that must be heard," Locust said quietly as he placed a hand upon Protector's shoulder. Looking up, Locust spied Toad, gawking, with his arm still up in a defensive posture.

"Gather all of the skulls in this place and place them around here, just so!" Locust commanded Toad, pointing and gesturing. "Gather wood and make a large campfire here!" Locust yelled at the Helpers.

"Many have been cooked and broken," Toad croaked as he picked one up and stared into its blackened face.

"Gather them all, especially those," Locust instructed. "We must stay here and answer the voices."

That night, they sat up late and talked around the campfire. Protector told them many things he had not spoken of before. He spoke of this place where they are camped, the place of his grandfather's youth, of the carnage that happened here, of his tribes' exodus from this place. He spoke about the Pivanne and the battle at Skyhouse, of Kolichiyaw, the old man, of his mother and his father, and of his exile from Skyhouse. He told them many things and they listened. Then Locust stood up. "It is time we make a ceremony," Locust announced.

Mumbling inaudible words, he went about his rituals. He presented and then spread corn meal in all four directions. He placed feathers in each of the four directions and threw green spruce upon the fire. A liquid was prepared and placed by the fire to warm. Toad and the Helpers were sent a short distance away to act as spirit guards. Locust picked up the pot of liquid by the fire and drank deeply from it. He offered the little pot to Protector without looking at him.

Protector looked at him and then at the liquid. He did not reach for it; he remembered the last time he visited the spirit world and he did not want to go there again, especially here, in this place.

"I have drunk of the liquid. Must I alone listen to the voices that have reached out to you?" Locust asked.

Protector hesitated, looking down, and then took the liquid and finished it.

They sat by the fire late into the night, waiting, not talking, just waiting. The crackle of the fire and the distant rattle of Toad's and the Helpers' gourds were the only sounds. The skulls placed round about seemed almost animated by the flickering campfire light. Protector was a bit uneasy as he looked from one skull to another. He thought that Toad and the Helpers had drifted off to sleep, as he had not heard their rattle gourds for a while. Then, something caught his eye.

The dirt by the fire, just there, was beginning to move. Yes, there it was again! *Definitely something digging up out of the earth, a snake perhaps*, Protector thought. Now a tentacle came up out of the widening hole; it was reddish brown and in sections. It was not a snake. Now the earth was moving much more; something large was coming out!

Protector, wide-eyed, looked at Locust. Locust, mouth agape, had already seen it and was sitting motionless, hypnotized by the spectacle. Suddenly, the ground erupted and an *ant*! An enormous *ant* burst forth from the earth!

Half as large as a man, the thing was out now and it struck a pose in front of Protector and Locust. Protector moved quickly to get his bow, which was behind them, leaning against a ruin wall. He strung an arrow and aimed it but was blocked by Locust, who had risen and walked in front of Protector, hands and arms out to stay his arrow.

"Do not harm him," Locust said. "He is sacred to the people. I have told you the stories of that long-ago world where his kind took us in and saved the people."

Protector hesitantly lowered his bow but did not put it down. He was not so sure that this monstrosity was of the same beings in the stories of that ancient world.

"You are wise to remember those days, human!" said the creature, waving one tentacle in the air. "Wise to remember and to tell the story of those days for others of your kind to know and to keep."

"How is it that you speak our language?" Protector found himself asking.

"We have no need for language but speak it I must for it is the only way that your kind may understand."

"What is it that they call you?" Protector asked, instantly regretting his question.

"We have no need of names," said the creature. "In all the worlds, you are the only creatures that need such things. Even we had to give you a name. We called you Mud Heads, for the earth would coat and dry upon you until it made your skin crack and bleed." The creature pointed one long tentacle at them and continued, "Deep in the bowels of the earth, you lived with us protected from certain death here in the above world. Nourished and cared for like babies until it was time for you Mud Heads to emerge into a new world to continue your journeys on your path of life. We have not seen you since, having no need of this place. Why does the Creator call us now to this spirit world to speak to and guide the Mud Head they call 'Locust'?"

"I am the one called Locust," Locust said as he stepped forward to address the creature. "But why have you been called for me, when it is the long dead human spirits of this place that need to be answered to?"

"Those spirits have been answered! If your ears worked, you would know this, for they call the younger one no longer. He *has* heard them and it is *they* who guide his footsteps now so that their seed, his own blood, may take root in fertile soil and grow again in the way that the Creator intended! No, Locust! I am here for you! What I have been given to tell you, I will do so in my own way."

With that said, the creature started moving one long spindly tentacle toward Locust. Locust stood firm but he was repulsed as the tentacle came near his head and he flinched, turning his head to one side as it came into contact with him.

"Stand still, Mud Head!" said the creature. "I have much to tell you."

Protector watched the pair as some sort of communication passed from the creature to Locust. They did not move; they were as if frozen. A strange buzzing sensation filled the air. In just a few moments, it was over. The creature released its contact with Locust and Locust fell to his knees.

"Are you alright?" Protector asked Locust as he caught him by the shoulders.

"He is well, young Mud Head, he is well," said the creature. "Tomorrow, you will continue your journey and you will know that you are on the true path. But remember, young one, remember the lesson of the ant—remember his lesson well."

The creature then walked backward until it reached the hole. Then in an instant, it was down the hole and gone, sealing the entrance as it went.

Locust sat all the way down with a thud, his hands on his knees, staring blankly. He said nothing. Protector was amazed at what happened. He walked to where the hole was, but there was no sign of it now.

"He is gone; it is over," Protector said, looking back at Locust, who was still staring blankly. "What did he tell you and what did he mean when he said to remember the lesson of the ant?" he asked Locust. Locust still said nothing; he just sat and stared blankly straight ahead. Strangely, Protector could hear the gourd rattles again. He stared off into the dark night and realized that Toad and the Helpers never really ever stopped. They were here, all the time, shaking their gourds, waving their feathers, and doing what they were supposed to do. It was he and Locust that left this place and entered into another world, a world not fully understood by Protector. He yelled for Toad and the Helpers to come in and go to bed. He looked once more at Locust, who was still staring blankly into the night. Protector found his mat and went to bed. He looked once more at the silhouette of Locust there by what was left of the fire, and then he found sleep.

The next morning found Protector being shaken awake by Locust. "Time to start moving. We have many miles to cover and I, for one, am anxious to leave this place," Locust said cheerfully.

Protector sat up on his mat and looked at Locust, bewildered. "I cannot understand you," Protector said. "Last night you looked as though you had seen your own death and now you are happy, happier than I have ever seen you."

"Some things are meant to be and cannot be changed, therefore, the wise man accepts his fate. Why not be cheerful about it?" said Locust.

Protector thought this all to be very odd. "What did the creature tell you?" he asked somberly. Locust stopped his hurried motions and thoughtfully looked off into the distance. "Every man has a purpose; he merely reminded me of mine," Locust said as though speaking to himself. "Every path has a beginning, a middle place to rest, and every path comes to an end. When the path is long, we tend to linger in the resting place too long. We forget the beginning and we avoid the end because we fear what lies beyond. The path itself has become the all."

Another answer like only Locust could deliver, Protector thought to himself. Questions answered by Locust only served to produce more questions. "Yes, and every path has a fork in it, and we may go in a different direction whenever we choose," Protector offered.

"Aha! But that fork we elected to take is the direction we were meant to go," Locust stated directly to Protector.

"Why do I even try!" Protector said under his breath. Protector put it out of his mind, got up, and readied himself for travel. Down the path, he paused and looked back, perhaps for the last time, at the sunbaked redness, the long dead place of his grandfather's father. He felt sadness and yet was eager for the days to come. His spring had become his summer, a new beginning or an end, it mattered not. He felt no fear for the days ahead.

Days turned into weeks, weeks turned into months, and soon Protector recognized the beginnings of river valley. There at that place, Protector looked at Locust and Locust looked back knowingly. There was no need for words.

"Let us sit here and talk," Locust said to the entire group.

Protector was surprised that Locust was giving him this opportunity to say goodbye. He assumed that when they came to his river valley, Locust would simply bid goodbye in his customary emotionless manner and walk away without so much as a last look. But in any case, Protector was glad to be able to say goodbye face to face with Toad, the Helpers, and yes, Locust.

Protector was the first to take a seat cross-legged, upon the ground. Toad and the Helpers came ambling over, with prompting from Locust, not fully knowing what was going on. Once they sat down, Locust selected a spot in the middle of everyone and sat down.

Protector began to speak but was interrupted by Locust.

"We have traveled far together. We have traded with many peoples. We have taught much and learned much. We have seen places of beauty and places of danger. We have met that danger and we have avoided it whenever we could. Up this canyon lies such a place. It is Protector's tribe that lives in this river valley," he continued. "They are of the people but have long since lost their way. Their eyes see but they are blind. They are full of hatred and fear and will kill us if they can. I go there now with Protector to place their feet upon the path. You, Toad, and you, Helpers, must go on to the winter place. The people there will make you welcome and help you through the winter."

At this, a low wailing started slowly and quickly built into a great crescendo of grief emanating from Toad's grimacing and tortured face.

"No! Noooo! Toad goes with you! Toad goes with you, Father. Please!" Toad pleaded, sobbing as he got up and ran over to Locust and wrapped his grotesque form around Locust's neck. It shocked Protector a little to witness this. It was not the first time he had ever seen Toad cry. He had seen him cry before, usually about some slight he had received from Locust. But he had never heard Toad call Locust 'Father,' before and it shed a new light on Toad's fragile soul.

Locust pried Toad's one pathetic gnarled arm from around his neck and sat him upon the ground. Toad sat there sobbing, head down, as Locust continued, "Each of us strays from the true path or finds ourselves resting too long in the comfortable middle place of their path. I have been led back to the true path by the Creator, who sent a messenger to Protector and me. He spoke to me and set my feet back upon the path. He removed the fog from my eyes and allowed me to remember the beginning and glimpse the end of my path. It is toward that end that I go now. It is because the Creator has let the sunlight from the next world shine upon my eyes for a moment that I go there happy and fulfilled."

With a great wail, Toad was upon his leg with a clasping vengeance. Locust pried him off again and picked up only his flute, leaving all the rest with Toad and the Helpers. He motioned for Protector to leave with him.

"Toad knows the way; make him leave with you now," Locust yelled at the gawking Helpers.

Protector picked up his bow and arrows and his pack. He followed Locust, looking over his shoulder at the sobbing Toad. "Walk quickly or he may follow," Locust said to Protector.

Remembering Locust's prophetic words, Protector caught up to the quickly striding Locust. "I go to live, or to die if I must, but I do not go to see any sunlight in the next world if I can help it. Why do you go? Do you think you will die? If you think that, then why would you go?" Protector asked Locust.

"The Creator did not show me my death; he only revealed where my path of life in this world ends," Locust said without slowing his pace.

"Why do I ever try!" Protector said aloud after a quiet moment of trying to understand the words of Locust.

They walked the river trail that led to Skyhouse. Before the sun was very high, Locust put the flute to his lips and began playing loudly. "Shhhh! Stop! They will hear us, they will know we are coming," protested Protector, putting his hand to the flute.

"Did you have a plan?" Locust asked, pausing. "Were we going to sneak up on them, all two of us?"

"No, we walk the river trail; they will see us coming," Protector said.

Slowly Protector removed his hand from the flute as he thought back to the days when he was 'Boy Who Watches.' He knew that Sityatki would have someone watching the trail.

"The village will be warned; Sityatki will be ready for us. The smoke will tell him that there are only two of us."

"Hmmm, too bad that there is no other way to get to the village other than the river trail you have told me about," Locust said.

"Another way to the village," said Protector, thinking out loud. "There is another way to the village! Well, almost to the village!" exclaimed Protector, remembering back to when he and old Kolichiyaw used the ancient ones' tunnel to bypass the river trail and come within sight of Skyhouse across the river atop the high cliffs. And yet, old Kolichiyaw had made it down those cliffs somehow. Perhaps he and Locust could get down the cliffs as well, but what then, even if they *did* make it down the cliffs.

Locust was right, it was time for a plan. He motioned for Locust to sit with him. He began to tell him everything he knew about the river trail, the tunnel, the village, the talking smoke, everything. Finally, after a long talk, they came up with a plan. They would bypass the warning system of the village. They would travel to the high place across the river from Skyhouse. There they would watch and wait for an opportunity to confront Sityatki with as few of his followers as possible. Perhaps Sityatki would go on a hunting trip and Protector and Locust would see him leave. They could then race across the mesa and, using the tunnel, could confront him when he did not have so many to back him.

They traveled the river trail the remainder of that day. Protector was on edge because he knew that they could encounter a stray hunting party from the village, but they did not for luck was with them. That night's camp was without fire and without much talk. Tomorrow they would reach the tunnel and then the rim country above the river. No more than half a day's walk on that mesa would take them within sight of Skyhouse.

"Ooohh," Locust moaned. "It is not easy sleeping on the ground without a mat. And I am getting no younger, fast."

"You should have at least taken your mat!" Protector said.

"I was in a hurry to leave. We were lucky he did not follow us," said Locust, referring to Toad.

Protector paused, thinking about Toad. Funny, he actually missed the pathetic misshapen, little creature. "It is time to go, we reach the tunnel soon," he told Locust.

They walked briskly along the river trail. Protector and Locust were able to wade across the river without swimming. There Protector filled his skin bag with water before he showed Locust the entrance to the tunnel. The entrance was even more overgrown than before with layer upon layer of sticker bushes. Finally Protector found the dark, dank entrance and he proudly stepped back to show Locust.

"Hmmm," murmured Locust, holding his chin and studying the entrance. "So you found yourself a pathway to the rim above, made by the Ancient Ones, I believe."

"Ancient Ones! Ancient Ones! Ancient Ones! Who are these Ancient Ones?" Protector asked. Old Kolichiyaw had also talked about them.

"There have been worlds other than the one we know," Locust answered simply. "They sometimes left a sort of map of these things," he said, stepping back out of the thicket and looking along the rock wall nearby. "Aha! Here it is!" he proclaimed, pointing to a carving in a shaded part of the rock face.

Protector left the entrance and walked quickly to the rock face to examine the carving, his brow furrowed with disbelief to discover something else he did not know about this area. The carving was of a line, curved and indented and straight—could be a trail or a river. It was marked three times here and there with small circles.

"What does this line represent, and these small circles?" Protector asked, his fingers on the carving.

"It has to be the river," answered Locust. "These small circles are the tunnels they made going down to the river from the mesa above. See how the tunnel at this place corresponds to this circle on the wall," he said, pointing to one of the circles carved in the wall.

These words took Protector back to a time long ago when an old man somehow found his way down impassable cliffs across from Skyhouse and lost his life attacking the Pivanne before a young boy could risk his own life doing the same thing.

Locust's sun-darkened slender finger jutted outward and landed on a carved circle toward the end of the rock map.

"And this tunnel shown here is right across from Skyhouse," Protector said, his eyes narrowing with new understanding. "Come, we go now," he said as he handed Locust a stick.

"What's this for?"

"Spiders," Protector said as he entered the tunnel.

The climb up the tunnel was the same as it had been those years before for a young boy who was now a man. The walk on top of the mesa was long and hot. They were not too far from the high place across from Skyhouse when they saw it.

"Look! Look there—smoke!" Locust said, pointing toward the mesa.

"It is smoke, coming from the high mesa, old Kolichiyaw's place. They are using the talking smoke to warn Skyhouse."

"Warn them? Warn them of what? Of us?" Locust asked, alarmed.

"No, no, I don't think so," Protector said as he strained to read the smoke. "One comes, river trail, one comes, only one."

"Who is it? The Pivanne, Headbangers?" asked Locust.

"Hurry! We must get to where we can see what is happening," Protector urged.

Half running, half stumbling, they finally reached the high place across from Skyhouse. They paused to catch their breath and then they slowly peeked over the edge. The village was in uproar. Many people were on the beach, yelling and pointing, looking down the river trail. A great commotion was making its way up the trail to the village. The commotion was coming within sight of Protector and Locust now.

The village warriors were dragging someone toward the village. Their captive was bound by rope and held away with long forked limbs. As they dragged their hapless victim toward the village, they encircled him and leapt about in a great shouting frenzy. Each time the captive would stumble and fall, two or three of them would rush in and jab him with pointed sticks until he got up and continued his tortured walk. Protector felt sick as he realized who it was. "It is Toad," he croaked. "They have him."

"Poor Toad! I might have known that he would follow. He will surely be killed," Locust said sadly.

"Yes, he will die, slowly and painfully if we do nothing," Protector said, looking at Locust.

"And what do you think we should do then? Go all the way back to the tunnel, and then back up to the village where we will surely join our small friend in bondage, that is, if he is still alive by then?"

"No! There is another tunnel here close by somewhere!" said Protector. "Remember the map carved on the wall near the tunnel we used? Old Kolichiyaw must have used it to get down to the river when he... when he—"

71

"When he died!" Locust finished.

Protector paused for a moment. He realized that if Toad received any help, it would have to come from him and only him. He got up hastily and began looking for the tunnel that must surely be here somewhere. *It could not be very visible, or else many others would know of it*, he thought.

There was nothing, nothing anywhere near the edge. Frantic now, he continued to search. Time was running out; he could hear Toad screaming. Then he saw it! A knoll of rock back a bit from the edge and overgrown with sticker bushes. He ran to it and began thrashing about in the bushes. Then, separating a particularly thorny clump with blood running down his face, he saw it—the tunnel!

"It is here!" he exclaimed excitedly, loud enough for Locust, still watching near the edge, to hear. "If this is the end of our path, then the Creator honors us, for what better way to die than to do so trying to help the most pathetic and least of all of us who walk his world. Surely you must have felt this way when you saved him from certain death when he was that deformed baby about to be thrown to his death by his own people. Won't you please come with me now?"

Locust seemed not to hear, for he still just stared over the rim. Slowly, he turned and faced Protector. "It is not my purpose to die at the hands of these lost ones. It is not the end of my path as foretold to me by the Creators messenger. Someday you will understand."

Silently staring at Locust, Protector paused only for a moment before he turned and disappeared into the blackness of the tunnel.

The tunnel was not as vertical as the other one, although Protector had only enough room to crawl on his hands and knees. Protector carefully felt above and found that the tunnel was getting larger. He continued on, disregarding fear of spiders and unseen animals, until he found that he could now stand all the way up. Soon he saw a faint light in front of him—it was the opening at the other end. Protector separated some of the thick bushes and saw that it was not too far above the river and was directly across from Skyhouse. Drawing a deep breath, he burst through the thick brush and leapt into the river below.

Protector was immediately immersed in the deep channel which had always run on that side of the river. His bow was secure over his head and one shoulder, but he forgot about the arrows, most of which had floated away in the strong river current. He swam about half the river until his feet could touch bottom. When he stood in the water and started walking to the shore, he could see that Sityatki and his warriors had stopped tormenting Toad and were taking note of his approach.

When he was a few shallow steps from the shore, Protector could see the warriors starting to string arrows. If it came to a fight, which he knew it must, he figured that he had one slim chance, to shoot an arrow and run, again and again, leading the warriors on a deadly chase where he could pick them off one by one, using his superior speed and ability with the bow.

Protector reached for an arrow of his own and found that he had only one left. Fear leapt into his heart and he tried not to reveal his disadvantage was even greater than he anticipated.

Toad raised his head and saw Protector. Blood and saliva were running down his face and dripping off his chin. Even through the pain, Toad's face broke into a bloody grin of recognition and hope. A wretched wail emanated from his mouth as he attempted to call out to his friend.

"Sityatki!" Protector yelled at the group of warriors who were just out of killing range with the bow. "Sityatki!" he yelled again, this time louder. "Come out and face me! Face one who can fight back, you coward!"

"Who are you?" came a yell from the crowd. "Who are you?" came the yell again.

Protector squinted over his slightly lowered bow and his one arrow to see the owner of the voice, but he could not quite see. Somehow, though, he knew it was Sityatki.

"I AM THE ONE YOU ONCE KNEW AS BOY WHO WATCHES," came Protector's answer.

"Boy Who Watches? Boy Who Watches?" yelled Sityatki as he strode forth out of the crowd of warriors who were murmuring among themselves at this revelation.

"YOU ARE THE COWARD! RAN OFF FROM THIS PLACE MANY MOONS AGO AND TOLD NOT TO RETURN, ELSE YOU WOULD DIE!" Sityatki yelled. "Die like your father did, before he gave me this amulet," Sityatki continued sarcastically as he sneered and fingered the sandstone eagle amulet which hung around his own neck.

Hate replaced fear in Protector's heart as his free hand went instinctively to the matching amulet around his own neck and he absorbed the full meaning of the words he had just heard.

If only one person died this day at the end of his one arrow, he grimly resolved, then it would be Sityatki. But he was still out of good range for the arrow, somehow, he must get just a little closer. Just then, Sityatki turned to the warriors and shouted: "GO FOR HIM NOW AND KILL HIM! KILL HIM LIKE THE DOG HE IS!"

The warriors moved en masse toward Protector but stopped in their tracks upon hearing 'It'! 'It' was a monstrous loud sound seemingly coming from the entire face of the cliff on the opposite side of the river. The sound came from the cliff face, like nothing anyone had ever heard before. Louder than the loudest thunder; it made the men weak in the legs with fear. Even Protector was taken aback by the loud and strange sound, until it dawned on him what it was.

"Locust! Locust is playing his flute in the tunnel!" he whispered to himself.

Somehow the shape of the tunnel, small at one end and large at the other, was amplifying the sound of the flute to an extraordinary degree. Protector could even recognize the tune now, although it was hideously loud.

"I AM LOCUST

I AM LOCUST

I BRING SEEDS

I BRING SALT

I BRING HONEY

AND BLESSED CORN MEAL

ALL FOR YOU"

"Father! Father!" cried out Toad when he figured out what the sound was. Protector glanced at Toad's agonized face and realized that this was his only chance. As quietly as he could, he strode forward with his bow and his one arrow until he could see Sityatki clearly and was in range.

All eyes were turned toward the cliff face, even Sityatki's, until it was too late. Sityatki's head turned from the cliff face and for a brief moment his eyes locked with Protector's eyes. And in that same moment, he saw the arrow flying toward him.

The arrow found its mark and Sityatki did not suffer.

Just as suddenly as the sound from Locust's flute had begun, it stopped in that very instant.

As vindicated as Protector felt, he knew that this was probably only the beginning of his fight. He spotted a quiver of arrows on the ground at the feet of one of the warriors, and he ran to try to get it. He quickly covered the distance to the quiver and reached out to get it, hoping that the group was still immobilized by the sound of Locust's flute. As he reached, he was pushed to the ground and surrounded by dozens of chattering warriors.

What is this? They were not attacking him; they were patting him on the back; they were helping him up! They were telling him a dozen stories all at once.

Moonflower, the beautiful young girl of his youthful memories, came running and hugged his waist.

Three of Sityatki's closest cronies slyly faded into the background, and when they were far enough back, they turned and ran down the river trail, the same river trail that Protector had run down to exile so many years before.

Apparently, life had not been so good for the village since the day that Sityatki had taken control and Boy Who Watches was sent away.

Stories of cruelty and bad decision and, yes, even murder, overwhelmed Protector. Protector's own family was killed. Protector was now honored and revered as a liberating hero.

The sun was not yet high when the group of young warriors from Protector's village approached the Helpers, who were still right where Protector had last seen them—far down the river trail where Protector's river canyon began. They had not moved since Protector and Locust had left, as they were also abandoned by Toad.

The Helpers were frightened at first, but the young warriors brought them fresh food. They told the Helpers the tale of Protector, who had returned to save their village, and now bade them welcome to follow the warriors to their new home to spend the rest of their lives with Protector's tribe.

At Skyhouse, sometime much later, Toad was sitting on a deer-hide blanket near a warming fire. He was entertaining several young children of the tribe with woven figurines he was creating. He stopped now and looked across the river at the cliff face, as he frequently did, and remembered.

Skyhouse

They never found Locust. Protector swam across the river, soon after his reunion with the tribe, and made the perilous climb to the tunnel opening to search. He searched through the tunnel and to the mesa above and beyond. But all he ever found was a flute, a small bag of salt, and a pouch of seeds left by Locust, his legacy to the one he knew as Protector.

Protector was drawing on the cliff face in the large room at Skyhouse. He was illuminated by torch light and his audience included many of the tribe, including adoring Moonflower. As he dipped his finger in the small paint bowl, he continued his drawing.

"This," he said as he drew a stick figure of Locust, in full head-dress with his flute, on the wall, "is the new name of our clan. In the spring, we will leave this place and we will return to the true path, and you all will have much to learn."

"Yes, Teacher, we will learn."

Across the river, one stared down from the high mesa. One with markings on his face and teeth filed to a point.

Many years later, the teacher would return to this valley after many accomplishments and many adventures.

And he would be buried there in that opening across the river and the opening would be walled up. He would be known by the last name, "The Great Man."

But that is but the end of the rest of the story.

BROTHER DEVIL

MICHAEL NALIBORSKI

PREFACE

Funny how some images or memories, although they be brief, will haunt you throughout your life. One of my most vivid memories is of a boy at the carnival when I myself was a boy. He had hair all over his face and apparently most of his body. For a brief moment our eyes met and I could sense loneliness and trouble.

The image of that boy in my memory and memories of my youth living in the desert of New Mexico with my family, riding horses, hunting on foot miles away from anything. Memories of my grandfather, who had a small ranch in the wilderness area of west of Payson, Arizona. He used to lead trail rides for dudes along the Mogollon Rim. All those images and memories played a part in the story you are about to read.

BROTHER DEVIL

I remember the night that I met the devil, least ways that's what Grandpa called him. I call him Dev now.

I was just a young'un when I woke up to Grandpa's hollering in the middle of the night.

"I see you, Devil, I see you out there! You give me half a shot and I'll make you a dead devil," Grandpa yelled as he fired a shot from his double-barreled shotgun.

Well that did it, that shot really woke me up—not just half woke up. I rolled out of bed and squinted out the window. Grandpa was on the front porch holding up a lantern, but that just meant that you could see him a lot better than what was out there in the bushes. He was holding that lantern as high and as far out as he could, trying to see something out there in the bushes. Then Grandpa stepped off the porch and was walking out away from the house.

That was it for me. I lit my lantern and slipped my boots on. Out the door I went, onto the porch, then out into the scrub bush with my lantern held toward the lantern light that was about a hundred foot away that I knew to be my Grandpa's.

When I got to where Grandpa was, he was holding his light and looking at something lying there on the ground. What was it? I wasn't certain at first. Wasn't enough hair to be a lot of critters I knew of; it was dirty—real dirty—with a mat of longish hair at one end, full of burrs, and shorter light hair all over the rest of its body. It was bleeding but I could see that it was still alive. Its chest was rising and falling and I could hear it breathing. Then it dawned on me—it was human, not an animal, it was a kid about my size.

Grandpa was loading new buckshot shells into his shotgun and I could see his hands were a-shaking. I think that was the only time, that I remember, ever seeing Grandpa scared.

"Boy, that thing ain't hit real good, it ain't near dead. Stay away from it now and I'm gonna finish the damn devil," Grandpa said.

Instead of moving away, I fell on my knees by the wounded boy. "Grandpa, don't kill him, he's a boy like me! He needs help."

I shocked myself. I didn't ever speak back in any way to him. I learnt early not to do that. After Grandma died and was no longer around to speak up for me. I learnt, learnt good. But now was different; I couldn't let him kill the boy, I just couldn't.

"That thing is the Devil, not a boy!" Grandpa yelled, pointing down at the boy. It must have been the tears falling from my eyes onto the boy that changed his mind about killing the boy. Grandpa's eyes softened a bit and he grabbed his chin in thought. "Chances are, he'll die anyway," he said to himself. "Put him in the hog barn, John," he said to me. "In the hog pen with the wire. If he dies, he dies. You take care of him if you care that much. I'll have none of it." With that, Grandpa turned and walked into the house, slamming the door behind him.

I dragged the boy into the barn. He was bleeding real bad. First thing I had to do was stop the bleeding. I took my nightshirt off and tore the bottom of it off for a bandage. Then I ran and grabbed

Grandpa's homemade horse liniment and doused his bleeding leg with it. The boy howled like a coyote cause that stuff burns like fire on an open wound. I wrapped my bandage around the leg wound as the boy lay there arching his back and wincing in pain, his arms up near his head. Hands clenched till his knuckles turned white, despite the dirt. Well, I dragged him on into the empty hog pen and threw a horse blanket down for him to lie on.

I stayed there in the barn all night with him, not that I wanted to but every time I tried to leave, he would howl like the devil Grandpa thought he was. I was afraid Grandpa would come and finish him off for sure.

I fetched him water in the morning; he drank it like a dog. Went up and got him bread from the house when Grandpa wasn't looking; he ate it so fast he got choked on it.

That's how it went, day after day, taking care of Dev while trying to keep up with my chores at the same time. Dev didn't make it easy either. His toilet habits left a lot to be desired. Many times I felt like just leaving that hog pen open and letting him go back to where he came from. So one day I did. Whatever happened couldn't be as bad as this.

After I left the hog pen open, I was scared and sad at the same time, knowing as I walked back to the house that I probably would never see Dev again—hoping I would never see him again. Then I was at the house, looking out the window, waiting for him to run out of the barn and disappear out in the bush.

If you could call it running, that is. Dev never did heal up real good. That one leg never did move right again after Grandpa shot him. After an hour of looking out the window, and Grandpa still hadn't made it back from town yet, I just had to go back and see if he was still in the barn or not.

He was there alright, right there in the hog pen with half a dozen dead chickens, or their parts, lying all around him. He smiled at me with a huge bloody satisfied grin. Blood and feathers were all over him.

Just then I heard Grandpa's rig coming up the road. Not knowing what to do I gathered up chicken parts and feathers haphazardly and threw them into the chicken roost area. Maybe I could blame a fox or something. Trying to look calm, I went out to meet Grandpa and unhitch the horse for him. Gramps jumped down and grabbed a large sack out of the rig. "Got us this store-bought chicken feed, cheap," Gramps announced. Gramps had the sack and was headed for the barn. My heart jumped in fear of what he would find out about the chickens. I couldn't move. I just stood there with the reins in my hands, staring at the barn.

Then here he came! His eyes were bugged out and an awful grimace was on his wrinkled face. "The Devil! The Devil! That's what he is, just like I thought, he's a devil. And I'm gonna kill him sure!" Grandpa screamed as he ran for the house to get his gun.

Quick as a whip, I dropped the reins and ran for the barn. My god, it was the devil, hanging like a monkey from the top of the hog pen, blood still dripping from his blood-stained teeth. He was looking at me and growling, like he often did when Gramps came near him.

My mind raced. *What to do? What to do?* Too late. Here came Grandpa through the barn door, with his gun. "Stand back, boy! I'm gonna kill the devil. Stand back I say!" Grandpa yelled. I ran and got to Gramps and pushed the shotgun up just as he fired. It was enough so that he missed Dev. I had never got in Gramps' face 'bout anything before, much less anything like I'd just done.

Well it must have shocked Grandpa cause his wild-eyed attention was all on me now. He knocked me down on the ground and was coming at me all bug eyed and crazy looking, holding his gun like a club. Suddenly, Dev was on Gramps' back and he had bitten down hard on his neck. "AH-EEE!" Gramps yelled as he dropped the gun and started twisting around and around grabbing at his neck! Blood was squirting out of his neck when he finally managed to throw Dev off of him.

"They'll hang him. They'll hang him. You wait and see! Grandpa yelled as he staggered to the wagon that was still hitched up. Holding his neck with one hand and the reins with the other, he headed off to town in a cloud of dust.

I was in the doorway of the barn on my knees watching Gramps disappear. I was in a daze of disbelief when I felt arms around me—it was Dev. I looked at Dev and he looked back at me and I knew I was all he had. And, in a way, he was all I had. I couldn't let them hang him.

I went up to the house for some stuff. I got my camping gear and a blanket for Dev, my Stevens single-shot .22 and some ammo. I would've got Gramps' double-barrel shotgun as well, but it put me on my butt every time I ever fired it. I saddled the only riding horse Gramps owned and slung the bedroll and pack on the back of it and mounted up.

I spent quite a bit of time trying to coax Dev up on behind me but he would have none of it. Finally I figured out that he would trot along behind me just as easy as a whistle. So off we went—where, I didn't know. But we headed west toward Arizona territory, I reckoned. Maybe to Flagstaff or Green Valley. I had heard Gramps talk about the area once. It wasn't hot and desert there like the ranch. There are trees there. Maybe Dev and me could make a shelter of some sort and hide pretty good.

I knew Gramps would be looking for us, aiming to hang Dev and maybe me too. How hard he would look, I didn't know. Might be he wouldn't follow us at all, but I knew better. By nightfall we were further than I had ever been from the ranch when we stopped for camp. There was no water for the horse and I didn't want to give him water from our canteen, so we would have to find water tomorrow for sure. I cooked up some of the bacon that I took from Gramps' smokehouse. Offered Dev some, but he turned his nose up to it. I built the fire up pretty good, then I fell into a deep sleep. In the morning I got up, stretched, and was surprised to see Dev eating something! Was it bacon? No, no, it was a rabbit that he had caught somehow and he was eating it raw. Don't guess he'd ever get over that preference of eating critters raw—didn't understand it myself. Dev turned his nose up to fried bacon, then he would go and eat something that would make a Billy goat puke.

"Dev, that's gonna make you sick," I said to Dev as I offered him a piece of bacon, from the night before, with my outstretched hand. "John, you eat?" Dev said back to me, offering me what was left of his torn-up rabbit.

Well you could've knocked me over with a feather. I never heard Dev say a word before. I just stood there with my mouth open and my hand still extended with the piece of bacon. "John, rabbit good," Dev said. "Yes, yes, it is good, rabbit is very good, Dev. But it's even better cooked." I grabbed the rabbit carcass from Dev and quickly broke off a hind quarter and stuck it on a stick to roast over the still smoking fire.

Dev sat there with his mouth open and quietly watched as I built the fire up and roasted the rabbit. I offered it back to Dev on the stick. Dev just looked at it then back at me. I took a bite of it. "Mmmm… rabbit good," I said, mocking the way Dev spoke. Truth is, it wasn't near as good as the bacon. Slowly Dev reached out and took the rabbit, took a bite of it, and started chewing. A huge grin spread over his face. "Rabbit good. Rabbit more good," Dev said, grinning at me. "Yes, Dev, rabbit is good. Rabbit more good cooked," I replied.

We shared rabbit that night, and we shared something else, a feeling, a feeling that real brothers have. A feeling of family that I longed for. A feeling that I haven't had for a very long time. Not since my mother died and the town people took me to live with Gramps, since there was no daddy around.

Back at the ranch, Grandpa Kelso finally arrived. He was still in his rig. His neck all bandaged up. He was leading eight men on horseback, including the deputy sheriff. He had talked them into believing his exaggerated tale of the demon that had attacked him and turned his grandson against him.

"John, John Kelso, where are you, boy?" Gramps yelled. "You there, look in the house. Someone look in the barn," Gramps yelled at the men, and they did cautiously, being full of liquor bought by Gramps and also full of tales of the blood-sucking demon spun by Grandpa Kelso. "Nobody here," a barfly named Chino said. "They done flew the coop." "They took my horse and some other stuff too. Who's riding them down with me?" Gramps announced.

"Hold on there, Kelso, your grandson is just a boy. And I hear this other one you call a devil is a boy even younger," Deputy Jon Stinger said. "I'm telling you, that one IS THE DEVIL! And it's twisted my grandson's mind. They stole my horse. That's against the law no matter what their age is. You, Deputy, are bound by the law to go after them."

"I'm bound by the law to do something, all right," the deputy said. "And what I think I'm gonna do, Kelso, is ride right on back into town, and in the morning I'm gonna send telegraphs to all the towns they may come to and alert the authorities there to pick them up if they show up. What I'm not gonna do is ride off, God knows which direction, without supplies, after a couple of kids on a horse, running away from a crazy old man. An old man who has blood in his eyes and I'm not so sure is all that innocent in this whole thing. Besides that, you don't even have a saddle horse to ride anywhere and chase anybody down, Kelso," the deputy said, almost laughing.

"Go on then! Go on back to your blasted town and send your blasted telegraphs! I'll take care of it myself!" Grandpa Kelso yelled at the men. The men all rode back to town along with the deputy sheriff, but not Grandpa Kelso.

Grandpa Kelso methodically went about gathering stuff up and throwing them into the wagon. Sundown found Grandpa Kelso driving the wagon westward. The ranch he had built and lived on for so long, his ranch, ablaze behind him, silhouetting him, burning by his own hand. Grandpa Kelso did not look back. He had a crazy look on his face, eyes bulging in unreasonable rage. He was driven by something unnatural to find John, his grandson, and the demon that is with him.

Me and Dev got up early the next day and traveled more than half the day when we found some water for the horse. As the horse drank his fill and I loaded our canteens up, I could tell that Dev was wanting to do some hunting there, but I kept thinking about Gramps. I knew that he had a crazy side to him and I thought that he could be on our trail for sure. So I pushed on, walking and leading my horse and followed by a disappointed Dev.

So it went, day after day, we traveled, always pushing hard. I was amazed how much Dev was talking and soaking up all the bits of knowledge I could give him.

He had come to liking his game cooked. Last night he even built the fire. And I have learnt from him. Things about hunting, which I never imagined. Things like how to smell, yes, how to smell! Dev could smell things like deer, coyotes, rabbits, and even water. I found out that I could too, to some degree, if I tried. One day, about noon, we came on a ranch house with smoke coming out of the chimney. I was for stopping there, to see if they were friendly, maybe getting a real meal if we worked for it. Dev was against it, but I finally convinced him to go down with me and see if they would give us some fresh water at least. I told him we could always take off fast, if we needed to.

I walked toward the ranch house, leading the horse. Dev followed twenty feet behind. He looked scared and ready to run. I tied the horse to the rail outside, walked up, and knocked on the door. "Who's there?" came a loud voice from the side of the house.

Dev took off, running like some kind of crazy jack rabbit, butt up in the air and down on all fours, his one hurt leg kinda dragging a little behind. I had never seen him run like that and it took me by surprise, even shocked me, and I stood there on the porch, looking with my mouth open. The man who was on the side of the house stood near, doing the same. A woman opened the door and stood there staring at the quickly disappearing Dev, just as we were.

"My, oh my," said the woman, still staring and drying her hands with a dish towel. "Can't say that I have seen anyone run that fast or in that particular way ever before in my life."

"That's my brother, Dev," I croaked, breaking the awkward silence. "My name is John, John Smith," I lied about my last name. "My brother is a little scared 'bout meeting new people."

"I'd say more than a little scared," said the man. "I never seen anything like that. Anyways, my name is Henry Durst. This my wife, Ruth." "Ma'am," I said, tipping my hat. "People call me Mema," she said back, still looking out toward where Dev ran with a concerned look on her face.

"We came looking for water for us and the horse. Maybe even something to eat, if we could work for it," I said. "We," Mema said back, "looks to me like there's only one of y'all left. But never mind that, I guess, you come on in this house, boy, and I'll get you something to eat." Mema put her hand on my back and led me into the house as she was still looking out the door toward where Dev ran. "Pa, would you feed and water their horse, then you come on in and get something to eat as well." Mema had stew already in the pot, and boy was it good! She no sooner got "Pa" and me served up good, then she was out the door looking for Dev. She had a plate of food in her hand as she wandered out amongst the scrub Juniper where Dev had run. Well she was out there somewhere for quite a while and I was getting worried, but "Pa" said she'd be ok, caring 'bout little animals and young'uns, that was just her way. Dev was a young'un and he sorta looked like an animal the way he ran off and all.

I sat there on their porch, not knowing what to do, but thankful and satisfied with my full belly when I saw a wonderous sight coming thru the scrub. It was Mema and Dev coming back, and good lord, he was holding her hand and trailing along beside her like a love-struck puppy! She led him right on up onto the porch and promptly hollered for Pa. "Pa, get that wash tub ready for bathing. This little, hairy one's got bugs; he's so dirty. And the other one has got to have a bath too."

Dev didn't seem to understand what she was saying because he just continued to stand there staring at her like she was the second coming. But I did, and I felt like running off the same way Dev had. The thought of this woman giving me a bath filled me with some sort of 'heart leaping out of my chest' terror.

Mr. Durst—Pa—got one of them great, big wash tubs, the kind that Grandpa used for dipping pigs and chickens. He filled it with water right out by the pump. He even heated some water in on the stove to take the chill off the bath water. I was pacing back and forth getting more and more nervous all the while. Dev was just sitting there on the porch staring at Mema all moon eyed. Directly, she finished what she was doing and came up on the porch, wiping her hands. Then she turned around without much thought at all and snatched up Dev like a duck on a June bug.

Out toward the washtub she marched with Dev in tow. Once there, she stripped Dev's clothes off with one hand while holding him with the other, just like she was yanking feathers off a chicken. Dev was no longer calm. He was getting wilder and wilder, trying to get away from her. And now he was starting to howl and make sounds like a wounded rabbit, all at the same time. It was raising the hair on the back of my neck so I took off and hid behind the barn. I was feeling pretty safe there. I don't think she saw where I ran. After a while, the howling and screeching stopped. I went to the corner of the barn to take a look, but I didn't see nothing. I turn around and YIKES! She was standing right behind me. "John," Mema said, "are you going to get in that bathtub willingly or are you gonna do it the hard way like Dev just did?"

She was standing there holding a dripping, naked Dev by his arm. I looked at Dev, standing all quiet, dripping, hair mussed up and wet. He looked so different. He was even a different color with all the dirt gone. Then he looked up at me and flashed a huge spreading grin like he wasn't quite right in the head or something. It all gave me the jumping heebie-jeebies.

"Oh yes, ma'am, I'm looking forward to it," I lied. "You won't have any trouble from me. I'll get right to it. Don't worry about me." Well I did it. Didn't like it but I did it. I was just about ready to get out of the tub when I heard Mema holler. "Don't forget your hair; you got bugs." Yeah, I had bugs. Didn't know what it was like to not have bugs. When they got too bad, Grandpa used to use chicken dip on me. I washed my hair.

When I finally came up to the house, I saw such a sight. There was Dev sitting in the rocking chair in front of the fireplace. He was wrapped up to his chin in a quilt and his mop of hair was mostly all cut off. He looked happy. Mema came up behind me and it gave me a start. "You're next," she said as she clicked the scissors open and shut. When it was all over at last, it did feel good in a strange way. Me and Dev were both grinning. Both of us sitting there by the fire and wrapped in blankets. It felt real good. It felt like… home.

The days passed smooth and sweet, each one better than the last. There wasn't any talk of us staying on—we just did. Dev helped Mema in the garden and learned to take care of the chickens without eating them or the eggs. I helped Pa. I milked the cows and I learned how to shoe a horse and irrigate apple trees. Stuff that Gramps never did. If I ever had my honeybee summer, this was it. At night Mema fussed with Dev, cutting his hair bit by bit off his body. Dev did have a tolerable more hair on his body than anybody I ever knew. I learnt how to read words from a book, well some words anyways. Enough so I could even read some sentences.

Then one day I was out in the fields opening some irrigation gates when I saw him coming from afar. He was a long way off but it was him for sure. He did look some crazier than I remember him. His hair looked more white and there seemed to be a lot more of it. Going every which way, not even a hat to corral it. And a nasty looking beard growing all down his neck.

I couldn't think. I couldn't even move for God knows how long. He was headed right for the house. The urge to run hit me like a lightning bolt. I threw down the shovel and I ran to the house faster than I ever ran anywhere. Mema and Dev were near the chicken coop with rakes when I got there. I grabbed Dev's hand and started yelling: "It's Grandpa! Grandpa's found us! We got to get outta here!" Dev just stood there with his mouth open, holding his rake in front of him. Mema was doing the same thing but with a frowny, puzzled look on her face.

"We got to go now, NOW! He's crazy. He will KILL US!" I said loudly. I grabbed his hand and started pulling him away. Mema grabbed his other hand to hold him there. "Wait a minute, hold on. Who's coming? Nobody is going to hurt you. You are safe here. This is your home now." Too late. I saw Grandpa coming down the road on the hill, less than a quarter mile away. He stopped the rig on the hill. He saw the ranch, but did he see us? Suddenly, he used the whip on the horse. The rig started flying down the hill, his crazy hair flying everywhere. Dev was looking at him too.

Dev screamed an agonizing cry of fear and alarm. He started pulling on Mema, wanting her to run with us. "Go! Go, Mema! Run, Mema, RUN!" He yelled, yanking on her arm. But Mema was resolute.

"No, Dev, no. I'll be okay. Whoever he is, whatever has happened. I will talk to him," she said. She turned and walked toward Gramps when he arrived.

I finally pulled Dev away from there and we started moving. Dev was crying, reaching one hand toward Mema. We were behind the barn now and I said to Dev: "Run, Dev, we got to run fast." His tardiness was interrupted by the sound of Grandpa entering the ranch area.

We run, oh how we run! It was too late to get a horse, my gun, or even water. *WE RAN!* Dev cried the entire time till we finally stopped to rest. "WE gotta have water," I said to Dev, my throat so dry I could barely talk. Dev just sobbed loudly, his head buried in his knees. "I have an idea, Dev. What if we was to climb old Rocky Point? It's too steep for Grandpa's rig to follow, and it's too steep for Grandpa to walk up. I bet there's some water in those rock pockets up there that we could get a drink from. We could see the house from there. Bet we could see if Grandpa was gone. Maybe even see Mema. What do you think, Dev?"

Dev looked up and stopped sobbing, his face all wet from tears. "OK, John, we go up there to look," he croaked. We started climbing. We heard shots that made us climb even faster. It took quite a while to get up there, but finally we made it just before dark. No way could Grandpa follow us up there. We were safe for a while.

Then we saw it—smoke! The ranch was burning; we watched it all night huddled together against the cold. Toward morning we could see that it was all gone, burnt.

"We gotta go down there and find out what happened, Dev." Dev was stone faced, no more tears. He stood up, matter-of-factly, and started down the hill. I quietly and grimly followed.

We found them both there at the house; they were dead. Blown apart by a shotgun, Grandpa's shotgun. We buried them, best we could, right there in the front yard. We piled up rocks on top and made two crosses. I found two pieces of unburnt flat wood and made letters, one for Mema and one for Pa. Don't even know if they had family. If they did and if they ever came there, they would see what became of them. During all this, Dev was not crying. He went about helping me bury them—no tears. Maybe he was just scared, like me, that Grandpa would come back and kill us both.

Time to leave this place. This place that could have been, that was, home to us. There was little said between us. Horses were gone, and the other animals turned loose, burnt up, and dead. There was water and I found a canteen, a flint and steel, and a knife. My heart was heavy and I wanted to cry but not as we set off walking, following Grandpa's tracks. We were still headed west.

Why we kept following Grandpa's tracks, I did not understand. I didn't want to catch up to him. I kept suggesting to Dev that we turn off of his track and head south, or north or even back, but he ignored me and kept walking, doggedly following his track. Even days later when the track had disappeared, we kept going.

Is Grandpa going this way because he figures that is the direction that we headed? Did he even know that we had been at the Durst ranch? Did he see us? What did the Dursts say to him? Or did he simply kill Mema and Pa only because he is now as crazy as a shit house rat? I didn't know but we kept following.

Then one day, at sundown, we smelled smoke. Dev looked excited. I was filled with dread. Whatever Dev was going to do, I figured he'd do it in the morning. At least I had the night to think of what I'd do in the morning if Dev wanted to confront Grandpa.

Morning dawned, and I was filled with dread again and I was hungry. *Do I run? Run away from Grandpa? Run away from Dev?* I looked around and did not see Dev. Dev was gone. I looked everywhere but he was gone.

I wanted to run, but I didn't. I started moving quietly toward the direction the smoke was coming from last night. Fact was, I still smelled smoke and something else too—bacon! My God, bacon, just the smell of it made my stomach growl. Quietly, I made my way to the source. Funny how you can move more silently when you are hungry. How you can hunt better and I think even see and hear better. I finally got close enough to see and I saw Dev sitting by a cook fire and he's eating. Eating from a plate.

"Hold it right there," a voice from behind me said. I freeze. The closeness of his voice startled me. "People usually don't have much luck sneaking up on me," he said. "That one over there eating did though. Don't know quite what he is, maybe Indian. Weird looking little feller don't talk much. Maybe you do. What's your story?"

"That's my brother. His name is Dev, my name is John. We were following my Grandpa, he's in a wagon. Have you seen him? He's crazy looking, crazy acting too."

"Yeah, I seen him alright. Your Grandpa? Wouldn't it be his Grandpa too?" With my head down, I answered, "Well, not exactly. It's a long story."

"Guess you're as hungry as that one is," the man said." Come on then, you can eat too, if there's anything left." There was some left and my god was it good! Dev scarcely even looked up at me between mouthfuls.

After breakfast, I found out that the man's name was Polk, William Gladstone Polk. I told him the story about Grandpa and Dev and the Dursts, Mema and Pa.

Mr. Polk was looking at the ground during the whole story. When I was done telling, he spat and looked at me. "You should tell the law first chance you get, boy. People like your grandpa get a poster out on them. Makes it worth shooting them."

I thought for a bit about his statement and then answered him. "We can't go to the law, Mr. Polk. First thing they'd do is separate Dev and me. Likely they would put Dev in a cage after what Grandpa told folks back home about him. The way Dev acts sometimes ain't exactly ordinary, Mr. Polk. No matter what, we are brothers, least ways we claim each other as such."

"Quit calling me Mr. Polk. It we are going to be traveling together for a ways, just call me Butch. I've got a feeling that your grandpa is gonna be worth some money sooner or later. If you two are dead set on killing him, well I might be of some help to you."

I didn't have the gumption to tell Butch that I wanted no part of Grandpa, that it was Dev who was hell bent on following him. If Dev had caught up to Grandpa before we met Butch, Grandpa would have, most likely, blown him to pieces with that double-barrel shot-gun of his, just like the Dursts.

"Don't know how we're going to get anywhere with one horse between the three of us," Butch said as he saddled his horse the next morning.

"Dev don't need no horse," I said to Butch. "He runs along with the horse. Can't even get him on a horse. He likes to catch rabbits."

Butch stopped cinching and looked at me. "Catch rabbits? How the blazes does he do that?"

"He just runs them down and catches them," I told Butch, using my hands to illustrate. "Rabbit got all kinds of tricks when he's being chased. Sometimes rabbits will run from him with their ears up, then they'll tuck their ears down and run away in a completely different direction. But Dev is way smarter than a coyote or a dog. Winds up catching rabbit more often than not."

"Have you ever noticed his hands?" I continued. 'They're all thick and callused. That's from running on all four like some kind of animal." Butch just stood there looking at me all frowned up and puzzled. "I'm afraid you might be pulling my leg, John. You kids haven't been chewing on a little locoweed, have you?"

"Oh no, sir, you'll see," I said. "Locoweed will kill you if you chew on it. Won't it?" I asked stupidly.

"You'll be a little crowded, with the packs and all, but you can ride up here behind me. We'll let your brother chase rabbits if that's what he does," Butch said, reaching an arm down to help me up.

He was right, it wasn't comfortable riding back there, but thing is, it was a whole lot better than walking. And I could smell more bacon in the packs and coffee too. It sure did smell good.

Just then a rabbit jumped up and Dev took off chasing him. Butch stopped the horse and watched Dev intently.

"That boy is uncommon fast. But look how he drags the one leg sometimes like it's hurt."

"Been shot. Grandpa shot him," I said calmly.

"Didn't say nothing before," Butch said without turning around. "Your Grandpa shot at me too. He's a crazy one all right. That's why I'm pretty sure he's gonna be on a wanted poster sooner or later. That's how I make my living, boy, hunting bad guys and crazy ones too. I'm a bounty hunter. I get money for bringing them in dead or alive!"

I had heard stories about men like Butch, but I never seen none, till now. Grandpa had an old paper book in the outhouse once that he had got from somewhere. I'm not much of a reader, not then anyway. Gramps never let me go to school. But the book had pictures. Pictures of gunfights and gunfighters. They wore pistols in leather holsters, kinda low on their legs, with the holster tied down with a piece of leather, just the way Butch wore his.

I thought about Grandpa being killed. It made me sad deep down inside me. There was some good times with him and me and an awful lot of bad times too. Then I thought of Mema and Pa lying there all blown apart and I knew there was nothing about either of them that deserved that. I hated him and wanted him dead.

"Whoo-Eee! He's got one!"

My thoughts were interrupted by Butch hollering.

"Never would have believed it, but by golly, I seen it myself!" he yelled.

"Looks like we're eating rabbit, boys," Butch said.

Proudly, Dev came back carrying the rabbit upside down, still kicking.

"Yuk," I say under my breath.

"Well, sir, we promptly stopped early right there to clean and cook that blasted rabbit." The rest of the day Butch spent teaching

Dev how to shoot his six-shooter. What a grand time they had, sitting up targets, practicing quick draws, laughing and laughing.

Next day, Dev caught two rabbits right off the bat. Again we made camp right away to cook them wormy rabbits and shoot up a whole box of cartridges.

"Thought you wanted to catch up to Grandpa?" I said to Dev during a quiet moment between practice shots. Dev said nothing in reply as he was totally involved with that six gun of Butch.

"Sowbelly won't last forever," I announced. Butch squinted at me. "What?" he said.

"Sowbelly won't last forever. Specially the way you got it stowed in that pack. And rabbits have worms this time of year."

Butch holstered his gun and turned toward me.

"John, if you don't want to eat rabbit, then don't eat. And if and when we catch up to your grandpa, then Dev is going to deal with him like this." Butch pulled out a gun and shot cones off a pinyon tree. He hit five or six of them in rapid succession. He and Dev squealed with laughter and delight and went right back to their shooting.

"Shouldn't eat a rabbit in any month that doesn't have an R in it," I said half loud and walking away, giving up. I really didn't know what my statement meant for sure, cause spelling wasn't my strong point. I had heard it said before and it kinda gave me the last word.

Next day it was the same thing—rabbit again—while the sowbelly got hotter and more rotten and the beans went uncooked. I've got to admit that Dev was getting tolerable good with that gun tho, no longer than he had been practicing. Fact was he was unnatural good.

Finally we arrived at the town of Green Valley. Not much there; there's a general store, some houses, a lumber mill, a gun store, and an eating house. We were greeted at the store by a man, on the porch, with a gun.

"Strangers, what are you wanting, trouble like the last stranger through here?"

"No trouble, just some hard tack and cartridges. Maybe some dried fruit and Arbuckle coffee if you got any," Butch replied.

"We got all those things except the cartridges. You will have to go across the street to the gunsmith for them," the man on the porch said. "Trouble is, the store owner who was our leading citizen, got killed a few days ago. Killed by a crazy, murdering old man in a wagon. Left a wife and four children. People around here ain't looking too kindly at strangers right now."

All of our ears perked up at his words, knowing that it was Grandpa he was talking about. Butch never let on that we knew who he was talking about.

"I can sell you what you want though. I'm running the place while the widow and kids grieve," said the man on the porch. "Bear with me though; I'm not used to doing this." Then he took a hard look at Butch and added, "You have the looks of someone who knows his way around a gun."

"Make my living with a gun," Butch said proudly. "The legal way, that is."

"Figured as much," the man said. "You might be interested to know that widow is offering five hundred dollars to anyone who brings that crazy old murdering man strapped to the back of a horse."

Butch looked quickly at Dev then back at me.

"John, get all the things that we need," Butch said, tossing me a ten-dollar gold piece. "Dev and me will go across the way to the gunsmith."

I went inside the store with the man and he clumsily started gathering up the things that Butch had mentioned.

"Where are you headed with them two?" he asked. "West, just west I guess," I said. "Well, if you don't mind me saying so," he said, "you don't look like you belong with them. Are you related or what?"

"The boy is my brother," I lied again. "The man is just someone we met on the trail, headed west."

"Odd, that boy don't look at all like you," the man said. "You know, we could use some help around here, running the store and all. This ain't what I do normally. I'm the lumber man, I run the mill over there. Pretty sure that the widow would hire you and your brother to help out around here. She could pay thirty dollars a month and found for both of you."

"Gosh, that sounds good, mister. I'll talk to my brother about it."

I quietly mulled over what the man had said as he continued putting our order together. Three hots and a cot for both of us and a roof over our heads. That's got to beat chasing a crazed old man across the country.

Then, through the window, I saw Butch and Dev coming back from the gunsmith. First thing that I noticed was that Dev now had a gun, a six-shooter, tucked in his pants.

"Where did you get the gun, Dev?" I asked. "Where do you think he got it? I bought it for him. Did you get our supplies?" Butch asked.

"He's getting them, Butch. But listen, they're offering Dev and me a job here. We could live here, Dev. We could sleep in a bed with a roof over our heads. Eat good food, save our money. We could have a life here, Dev."

Butch looked aggravated. "We're going after Grandpa, John. We're going after him and Dev is going to kill him with the gun I just bought him. Then we're bringing him right back here and collecting five hundred dollars for his murderous old hide. That's what we're going to do, John. Now if you want to stay here to sweep the porch and pluck chickens then stay here. You will see us when we come back with your grandpa strapped to the back of a horse. Maybe we will toss you a dollar when we do. Now where are our supplies?"

"He has them on the counter inside, Butch," I said as he brushed past me.

It's just Dev and me outside now and I directed my attention to him.

"Dev, don't you want to stay here with me? It could be a good life for us. We could even get some books and learn how to read and do numbers and stuff. If you really wanted a gun, we could save up some money and get a .22 for you like I used to have."

Butch came out of the store with the supplies and brushed past me again to put them in his saddle packs. He took out the old, half-rancid slab of bacon and slung it on the ground in front of me.

"There's your bacon, John, if you want it so bad," he said sarcastically. Butch swung up into his saddle. "See ya, John. You coming, Dev?" He turned his horse and left.

Dev stood there staring at me. I reached out to him with one hand. "Dev, stay with me, I beg." Dev looked at me, sadly, I think, and then just turned and left, following Butch.

"I'll show you where you sleep. Then I have to go clear it with the widow. It will be okay. She listens to me most of the time about stuff." I was still watching the disappearing forms on the road but I heard the man's words.

The man walked over and stood right behind me in order to get my full attention. "My name is Jim Baker. People call me Piney. I take it that your name is John."

Finally I looked away from the road. "Yes sir, my name is John, John Durst." I don't know why I took that name as my own. It made me proud in a way. I really don't think they had any relatives. That name was a good name and it needed to live on. I needed a good name.

That's who I was from then on, John Durst. Every day I waited for Butch and Dev to come riding back. Days turned into weeks and weeks turned into an awful long time.

The widow and I got along pretty good. I was a good worker, she said. Before long I was running the store all by myself and help-ing Piney out at the mill. The widow, she taught me about words and numbers. She pretty much had to teach me those things with me running the store and all, but I like to think that she enjoyed teaching me. I discovered that I wasn't stupid about such things. The widow's oldest daughter, her name was Sally, was my age. Throu gh the years we became sweet on each other. It was pretty much understood that we were going to get married someday. Why I pretty much had for-gotten all about Butch and Grandpa. I did think about Dev from time to time though.

Our little town was growing and by and by we got a new black-smith shop, and then we got a post office, just like a regular town. When that happened, we had to change our name since there was already a Green Valley in Arizona. So we changed it to Payson, which was the name of a man who had helped our small town out some.

But along with all the good things came some things that weren't so good at times. Like the saloon that started operating near the edge of town. Mostly it was cattlemen who used the saloon to drink, smoke, play cards, and discuss business. They all had to work the next day so usually it wasn't a problem. But every once in a while, the wrong type would show up and the saloon would have trouble getting them out of there for they could shut down for the night.

On the rare occasion that they did have trouble, the saloon owner had a great, big guy that they called Little Nater to throw people out. This arrangement worked real good. It worked good, that is, until the day the Chacon gang came to our little town.

I had read about the Chacon gang in the newspaper that came once a month. Kinda figured that they were made out to be a little worse then what they actually were—nobody could be that bad. But they were here in our little town now and I found out that they were that bad, real bad.

The Chacon gang started drinking early at our saloon and they stayed late. They were still raising Cain long after time for the saloon to shut down, so Little Nater had to throw them out. Well he tried to throw them out, just like he was paid to do, but they shot and killed him. Little Nater wasn't even armed.

The saloon owner, Joe, ran out the back door of the saloon and came and got Piney and me up out of our beds. Piney, Joe, and me were in the dark, hiding behind some barrels across and down the street from the saloon.

"What are we going to do, Piney? Have you got a gun?" I asked.

"We could send Joe for help, but it would take days for him to get back if he goes to any place with a sheriff," Piney said.

"What about Round Valley Ranch?" I asked. "They have a dozen ranch hands, and they have rifles."

Piney nodded in agreement. "Joe, saddle up a horse down at the corral and ride for the Round Valley Ranch. Stay on the road, Joe, or you'll break that horse's leg."

Joe took off down the street in the dark. Then it's just me and Piney.

"John, I'll get my shotgun and I'll get you one too," Piney said as he left to get them, not giving me a chance to answer.

I stared out across the street at the saloon. They were literally tearing the place apart. A chair went through the window with a loud crash just as Piney came back with the shotguns and touched my shoulder. I didn't hear him coming and I jumped at his touch noticeably.

"Here," Piney said, handing me a double-barreled shotgun. "Know how to use it?" he asked me.

"I know how, but last time I fired one, it put me on my butt," I said, remembering back to when I was younger.

"Don't pull both those triggers at the same time," Piney said, "and you'll be ok."

"We planning on shooting them?" I asked with some fear in my voice.

"They done killed a man, John. I don't plan on being another corpse propped up on the saloon porch, on display."

The ruckus went on all night. Just before the sun popped up, it was light enough to see a little. A couple of them came out onto the porch and relieved themselves. Then another came out, even more evil looking than the others. He had a patch over one eye and a red bandana on his head instead of a hat. I knew from the descriptions in the newspapers I had read that this was Chacon himself, the leader of the gang.

"Get us some food somewhere," I heard him hiss to the one who wore half a tattered sombrero.

The one with the sombrero tore off running down the other side of the street. That filled me with dread. Sally was down that street somewhere. She was probably wondering what happened to me about now.

I didn't have much time to think about it. Sombrero was coming back up the street, already dragging someone kicking and screaming. It was Sally!

"Look what I have!" sombrero man yelled.

"Where's the food? Chacon yelled back.

"This is better," sombrero man said, admiring his prize.

"Oh my God, Piney, they have Sally! We have to do something now!"

Without thinking, I stood up with the double-barrel shotgun and started walking toward the saloon. I didn't know what Piney was doing. I was blinded by the fact that they had Sally and I must do something. My legs kept moving, kept walking toward them as if they had a mind, a will of their own.

It was getting daylight now as I walked toward them. Sally was trying to scream or tell me something but her captor had his dirty hand over her mouth. More of them were coming out onto the porch.

"Well, what do we have here? A hero, a hero is coming to save the young lady from a fate worse than death," said one of them in a very loud voice. They all laughed. They were coming out onto the street now, right at me. Chacon stayed on the porch.

The one still had hold of Sally and they were on the porch with Chacon. The others were in a line not too far from me. I finally thought of Piney and turned a little to see if he was there.

"What cha looking for, your buddy? He took off running down the street. I guess he had something to do," Chacon said. The others burst out laughing again.

"Let her go," I croaked.

"Or what?" one of the six in the street said. "You gonna kill all of us with your big old shotgun?" They all railed with laughter at this.

Suddenly their demeanor changed. They stiffened up and got quiet. Someone was walking up behind me. That's what they were looking at.

Was it Piney? I wanted to turn around and look, but I couldn't. I was scared out of my wits. Slowly my fingers found both triggers of that shotgun. I figured if I did manage to fire, I might as well pull both barrels at once.

"What are you doing here, Devil?" one of the six asked.

Devil? My mind was racing when the person behind me answered.

"Your boss, Mr. Chacon there on the porch, has a price on his head."

Could it be Dev? It kinda did sound like him, but I dared not turn around and look.

"You and I never had a problem before. Can't we work together, Devil? Ain't nobody in this stinking town worth dying for," Chacon said from the porch as he nervously started moving a bit.

"That might be, except for the fact that it's my brother you're aiming to kill," the voice behind me said.

"GUN EM DOWN!" screamed Chacon.

I don't really know what happened then for sure. But I do know that I pulled both of those triggers before I even leveled the shotgun at them. That shotgun recoil lifted me off the ground and then flat on my back six foot from where I was. Bullets were flying over my head like a swarm of bees.

I could hear some moaning and I raised my head to look. There were six men in the street dead or dying and one on the porch, the one who was holding Sally, with a hole between his eyes. Sally was standing there with her hands over her mouth, unharmed, and she looked stunned.

I stood up, still holding the shotgun. Someone walked up behind me.

He looked at the shotgun then at me. "I would throw that down. You never did tolerate them things very well anyway."

It was Dev! I got a good look at him now. He was dressed all in black and he had not one but two guns on his belt. He had long, thin dark hair all over his face and long hair on the back of his hands.

He started walking away from me as Sally ran to me and we embraced in the street amid the dead bodies.

"Where, where you going, Dev?" I managed to say.

"One got away. The one that's worth money, Chacon," Dev said softly.

"What happened to Grandpa?" I asked, speaking louder now as he walked away.

"I killed him. He killed Butch. Didn't bring him back."

Then he stopped walking and looked back at me.

"Goodbye, brother."

I stood there in the middle of the street, holding Sally, watching Dev disappear down the road. He was running now, with that same gimpy gait that he had before. I guess he never did take to riding a horse. No bedroll, no coffee pot, no frying pan. Just Dev, and his guns.

Sally woke me from my thoughts. "John, who was that strange man?"

"That strange man is my brother, Sally."

She stared at me with a quizzical, frowning expression, an expression that asked questions.

"It's a long story," I said, walking her away from the grisly scene in the street.

A few people were coming out now, talking excitedly and looking at the bodies. Piney glanced at me sheepishly as he passed by, still holding his shotgun.

An hour later, Joe and the men from the ranch arrived. The men from the ranch pitched in and buried the gang. I told them to take the guns that the gang had in payment; they were glad to get them. We decided to bury Little Nater near the top of the little hill, near where Mr. Brown was buried. The others were buried down the hill a ways with markers that didn't have names but said why and when they were killed.

John

Things kinda returned to normal then, except for the way people acted around me. It took me a little while but I finally figured out that they thought I had a lot more to do with gunning the gang down than what I had actually done. I must admit that I was flattered by it all and didn't bother to set the record right. I guess nobody was really looking, not Piney or even Sally, when all the shooting was going on.

It got a little too much to take after a while. People admired me, they talked about me and pointed. There was even talk of making me a marshal, the town's first. Sally looked at me differently. She was in a hurry, all of a sudden, to set the date of our marriage. The whole thing was based on things that weren't quite true—it made me uneasy.

Well, that feeling didn't improve because the next thing I knew, everybody started planning a big celebration. There was going to be a lot of food to eat, banners, music, and dancing. And, I was told, they were going to give me something and I should be ready to give a little speech. *Give a speech? What am I going to do now?*

I didn't have long to think about it because the very next day they started hauling tables out into the street and putting banners up.

The whole thing just kept going like a runaway wagon, and before I knew it, I was seated at the very head of all the tables that were lined up. Somebody gave me a beer and a big plate of food and more than one pat on the back. Then someone hollered for me to give a speech.

Well, I tried to shrug it off, I even yelled for more beer. In the end nothing worked; they wanted a speech and I hadn't thought of a lie to tell them. I was never much good at lying anyways, so I stood up and told the truth—the whole truth and nothing but the embarrassing truth.

But why was it embarrassing? I did face the outlaw gang. I did go out into that street to save Sally. I did fire that double-barrel shotgun, albeit to no effect, except to throw me backward onto my butt. I never told them anything different. They believed what they wanted to believe. I never told them anything. Maybe I should have.

After my little speech, you could've heard a chicken blink. Nobody said anything for a while, then finally, none other than Sally, my beloved, spoke. "Well, I don't know quite what to say. We've all been led to believe one thing and now we are told an altogether different story. I think we are going to have to think this over for a while." With that said, Sally sat down and things went downhill from there. People got quiet. There were no more pats on the back, no more free beers, no more talk of making me Marshal. The party was over and people just seemed to tolerate me from then on. Sally didn't come around much anymore, and when she did, there was no more talk of marriage. I didn't understand it, but that's what happened. Even Piney, the guy who ran off, treated me differently. Maybe I had some rethinking to do also.

"My God"! Dev said out loud to himself as he left town, where John stood in the street, watching him leave. "Are those tears? Am I crying?"

He had never cried before, and although Dev wasn't sobbing noisily like he had seen people do, there was wetness coming from his eyes and making the hair on his face wet. It was strange to him and yet, it was gratifying in a way.

He had curiously watched people cry before, usually involving the loss of a loved one, and now he was crying. He was crying because he was leaving John behind again. He had wanted to be near him, talk to him, even hug him. But he simply said goodbye and left him behind again to pursue Chacon. If he was crying, maybe he was more like other people than he thought.

He shook off these thoughts in his head. He wasn't like other people—he was different.

People called him devil; they called him Lucifer. They stared at him but they didn't dare laugh at him because he would gun them down, even if it meant goading them into drawing first.

He made his money hunting men wanted by the law. He had no time for people and feelings, and people didn't have time for him. Oh, they would buy him a drink and pretend they were his friend. Then they would talk behind his back while their women laughed nervously.

John called him his brother. But did he love him like a brother? Dev felt a connection there and he started feeling sad again thinking about it. No matter; he had business to tend to and he quickened his pace. He would catch up to Chacon in a day or maybe two because Chacon would stop at night to rest. Dev would not.

It didn't take long for Dev to catch up to Chacon. It was the next night when Dev started smelling Chacon's campfire long before he actually came upon his camp. It was very late at night, but Dev could plainly see Chacon's form on the ground near the fire.

Dev could see better at night than other people. Other people – was he a person or something else? He didn't remember his mother, didn't remember his father. He just remembered running wild out in the scrub bush; before that, nothing.

Dev tried not to think of his 'running wild' days. This was who he was now, the person he was now.

Dev crept silently into the camp. Chacon had no dog to warn him. Good. Dev sat on a stump facing the sleeping form. Dev's guns were not drawn but he had pulled his poncho clear of them. Dev didn't stick his guns in his pants anymore. He wore the holsters and guns that Butch had when he died, except that he wore them with the guns backwards.

"Chacon!" Dev said in a loud voice.

He had seen men who took a gun to bed with them, even slept with one in their hand. Dev was ready for anything like that.

"Chacon!" Dev boomed even louder.

Chacon was startled. He thrashed around in his blanket and sat bolt upright on his roll.

"Devil! How did you find me?" Chacon said.

"It wasn't hard; you leave a trail like a pregnant buffalo."

"What do you want?" Chacon asked.

"Stupid question, Chacon," Dev said back. "You're worth money so I'm taking you back."

"Money? I've got money right there in my pack. It's yours; take it."

"Oh, I'll take your money," Dev said calmly. "Your money, your horse, your gun, your rig, all of it. And I'll take you too, Chacon, for the reward, dead or alive."

Dev sighed. He had asked the next question before. "So, what's it going to be, dead or alive? Alive is a pain in the ass, but at least you don't start stinking before I get you back for the money."

His little talk was interrupted by Chacon making a sudden move for his gun, which was a couple feet from him. Quick as a blink, Dev drew both guns and shot Chacon just as he touched his gun.

Dev moved quickly over to Chacon to throw his gun out of his reach. Chacon was not yet dead and he choked out some words for Dev to hear.

"The gold is under the floorboards."

"Gold!" Dev spoke to Chacon anxiously.

"What gold? Which floorboards?" It was too late for an answer from Chacon; he was dead.

He dragged Chacon's body off a little way and started scrounging around camp for something to eat. He might as well have stayed there for the rest of the night and rest before loading up Chacon's body on the horse and hauling him somewhere to get the reward.

But where to take him? The nearest town was Payson, where he just came from, where his brother was. They could send a letter of verification and eventually he would get his money. But that meant he would have to hang around until he got it. Nope, that wasn't going to happen. Better take him to Prescott. He would be starting to stink pretty bad by the time he got him there, but he would still be recognizable to the county sheriff.

Dev rested good that night. He slept but didn't sleep, a sort of half sleep, where the slightest noise would alert him. But nothing came in the night to chew the face off of his prize and make him unrecognizable, robbing him of his reward money.

In the morning, he wrapped up Chacon in a blanket and tied him over the horse for the trip to Prescott.

It took a leisurely five days to get him to Prescott. Dev even had time to catch a couple rabbits to roast. All the while he kept thinking about Chacon's last words: "The gold is under the floorboards."

What floorboards, what gold? The last place that Chacon was on a wooden floor was in the saloon at Payson. *Could he have hidden gold there?* Dev thought to himself. Might be worth a trip back to find out but it would take some thinking. Dev couldn't just barge in and start prying up floorboards. Or maybe he could, but it was his brother's town. This would indeed take some thinking.

Prescott came into view on the afternoon of the fifth day and it was a relief for Dev to get rid of Chacon's body.

The county sheriff wanted Chacon's horse to pay for burial and he got it, since Dev had no real use for it, except to sell it. Dev said nothing about the money that he found on the body. And he said not a word to anyone about the gold 'under the floorboards,' spoken of by Chacon before he died.

Dev spent two days bending an elbow with the bootlickers and he was ready to head back to Payson in order to somehow check under the saloon floorboards.

Dev made much better time going back to Payson—the thought of the gold drove him. When he entered the town, something seemed strange. The people looked at him and then just went on about their business; nobody stared, nobody laughed.

Dev went straight to the saloon. He didn't really have a plan in mind, but he knew that he needed a drink.

Dev walked in looking at the floorboards. When he finally looked up at the bar, whom did he see? None other than his 'brother by choice,' John!

John, the only one at the bar, didn't turn around to see who came in. Dev silently walked up and stood beside him at the bar.

"Well, Mr. John Smith, this ain't quite your style, is it? Drinking in the middle of the day?" Dev asked.

John looked at Dev and jumped a little in surprise to see him standing there beside him. "Dev!" John said, shocked. "You're back."

"Can't I come back to see my brother?" Dev replied.

"I took the last name of Durst," John said in a lower tone, looking around a little nervously.

"Okay," Dev said. "John Durst, John Smith, or John Kelso, why does it matter? None of those names are wanted by the law."

"There is the little matter of horse stealing from Grandpa," John said.

"Doubt it," Dev said as he took a drink from John's glass of whiskey. "I haven't seen anything about it on postings. In my business, I check them all."

Dev then looked directly at John. "And no," he said, "I don't know how to read. I make people read them to me. Fact is, I need to know how to read, John. Maybe you can teach me."

"Takes more than a few days," John said. "Takes weeks, maybe months; it ain't easy."

Joe, the bartender, finally came out of the back and gave Dev a glass without hardly looking at him. It struck Dev as odd behavior—people generally stared at him more.

Dev filled his glass, killed it all in one gulp and then filled his glass from John's bottle again.

"I'm not here for months, John. I've got to make a living. I killed Chacon. I killed him and got the reward money for him. That's the kind of money that I make, blood money. That's what people call it, but it's more than a dollar a day, like most make. What kind of money are you making, John?"

"I'm not making any money, Dev. I got fired. Things are not going well, Dev. Lost my job, lost my girl, lost all respect in this town. I've lost everything, Dev. That's why I'm here, at this bar, spending my last dollar on a bottle. I don't know what I'm going to do, Dev."

"Why? You were doing great here."

Sighing deeply, John told the whole story to Dev as they sat there drinking.

"Aren't people wonderful!" Dev said, shaking his head. "I did the killing instead of you, so they turn on you. You were the brave one, John, not me. You out there, with that cannon of a gun, standing up to the Chacon gang. For what, to protect their stinking town?"

"Well, John, got a place to sleep tonight?" Dev asked, after more drinking.

"Guess not," John said with his head down. "Got that horse out there and my bedroll and not much else."

"Sounds good to me," Dev said. "Let's get out of here. Give us another bottle, bartender," he said, tossing money onto the bar.

Dev took the bottle from Joe with one hand and helped John to his feet with the other. Outside, Dev helped John up on his horse. Then John riding and Dev leading the horse, they headed out of town to camp and drink the night away.

Dev spread out John's bedroll on the ground and built a fire downwind. He got John, who was passed out, laid down. Then Dev squatted down by the fire to rest and think.

The next morning, John finally got up. He stretched and rubbed his eyes as he saw Dev squatting by the fire, roasting something on a stick.

"What's for breakfast, Dev?" John asked, although he strongly suspected that he knew what it was.

Dev looked up at John without moving his head. "It ain't rabbit, if that's what you're thinking. Here, try a piece, it will help your headache."

John took the piece of meat offered to him and tasted it. "Dang, Dev, your cooking has improved," he said. "And you're right, it ain't rabbit; tastes more like… bacon!"

"Wrong again, John. It's rattlesnake. Ain't nothing better for a hangover," Dev said.

"Rattlesnake!" John exclaimed as he spit out what remained in his mouth.

"Yes, John, it's rattlesnake. Did it taste good before you knew it was rattlesnake?"

"Yeah, I guess so," John said timidly.

"One more question," Dev said. "Is there anything else here to eat?"

John said nothing for a short while. "Give me some more of that snake," he finally said. "Got any coffee to go with it?"

"Nope," Dev said, "but I know where we can get some. Before we go get it, though, I'm going to tell you about something."

Dev laid it all out on the table to John. The gold under the floorboards, everything. He told John about his plan to go back and get it, though there wasn't much plan to it. Just simply that—go back and get it. And seeing how John was apparently without funds and without friends, he figured that John would help him.

John found it difficult to go along with 'the plan' immediately. He was torn between his loyalty to the town he loved and his brother. But it was a town that did not want or need him anymore. There was also the prospect of no funds and no plans for the future. With that, and his renewed association with his brother, who seemed certain that they could get the gold without killing anyone, he decided that he was in on Dev's plan.

After their snake breakfast and their talk, John saddled up his horse and they both proceeded to go back to town. When they arrived, a few townspeople noticed them and were talking and pointing.

"Oh," Dev said, "that's more like it. That's what I'm used to."

"Where are we going?" John asked.

"The saloon; we got business there," Dev said.

Straight to the saloon they went. Dev looked neither left nor right as they made their way there. People pointed and whispered in their little groups, but Dev seemingly did not notice them. John noticed them, however; he looked at each and every little group of townspeople, his former friends.

"Don't worry about them, John," Dev said. "Their talk doesn't bother me and it shouldn't bother you either. If one of them goes for a gun, then it will bother me."

When they got to the saloon, John didn't know what to do but Dev did. Straight in through the swinging doors he went and straight to the bar with John trailing behind.

"Bartender, you and these two bootlickers are going to have to leave for a while. My brother and I need to have a little private meeting and we don't need any big ears hanging around," announced Dev.

The two men at the bar happened to be Piney and someone John had never seen before. Joe, the bartender, heard what Dev had said but made no move to leave.

"Brother," Joe said, "you're the man who killed those outlaws?"

"That's right, and the killing might not be done around here if you three don't get out of here like I told you to," Dev said.

Piney and the other man at the bar just sorta looked at each other with their mouths open. Piney, after a pause, stepped back from the bar, put his thumbs in his waistband, and self-assuredly spoke, "Maybe you two should know, this here is 'Bird Dog Jones.' Bird Dog was deputy to Seth Bullock of Deadwood up in South Dakota. You've heard of him, haven't you now?" Piney said smartly. "Well, Bird Dog is going to be our law here in Payson and he might have something to say about you two killing someone."

Dev and John had not moved to the bar yet. Dev reached out one arm and separated John from himself a little bit. Dev then addressed the two men who stood side by side a step away from the bar and ten feet from Dev.

"Seth Bullock never killed no one," Dev said as he slowly undid the hammer loops on each of his guns. "And I'm pretty dang sure that his bootlicking deputy didn't either."

Neither man near the bar went for their gun at these words. Bird Dog was just standing there looking, and Piney didn't even have a gun. He was still standing there with his two thumbs in his waistband and smirking.

Then it happened, quicker than you could see it. Dev drew both guns out and let one bullet from each rip. The hats of both men flew off to the back of the saloon somewhere—a bullet hole in each. A small trickle of blood ran down Bird Dog's forehead and onto his nose.

"Sorry there, Bird Dog," Dev said calmly. "I didn't judge that your head was so pointy shaped. You better go put something on that."

Both men busted out of that saloon so fast that you would have thought that they were on fire; they were falling, stumbling, and looking over their shoulder as they ran.

"Well, looky there, John," Dev said. "They done forgot their bottle."

Joe, the bartender, was sneaking around the corner of the bar, intending to make a dash for it when Dev stopped him in his tracks with a word, "Stop." Joe straightened up and looked slowly at Dev. "Bartender," Dev said, "you get us two clean glasses and about four of those god-awful warm beers to go with this bottle that those two bootlickers ran off and forgot, then you go and get us two big plates of bacon and eggs and you bring 'em right back here to us. Do you understand?"

Joe nodded his head and began to move out toward the door.

"Bartender!" Dev said louder. "If you don't come back, I'll make a signal fire out of your saloon and I'll come find you."

"Don't do that, please, I'll come back. I'll come back with food," Joe squeaked. Then out the door he ran.

"Well now, it's a lot more pleasant in here now," Dev announced to John. "Let's do some drinking and eating."

John and Dev sat there drinking and waiting for the food for a short while.

"Guess what I've been looking at," Dev suddenly said.

John was pretty sure that Dev had not been looking at anything other than the whiskey bottle in front of them on the one little table in the place, but he played along.

"What have you been looking at?" he asked.

"I've been looking at that loose floorboard over there in the corner," Dev said as he pointed one hairy finger toward the corner. "And I think it's time that we got down to business."

Dev got up and ambled over to the loose board.

"Find me something to pry with," he said to John.

John went around the bar and found a wicked looking hand axe on the shelves and delivered it to Dev.

"Say that looks like it might remove some boards or even someone's head, now don't it?" Dev said as he went about hacking at the thick hog lumber planks on the floor.

Dev got six or seven of the big floor planks up without finding anything underneath when Joe appeared at the swinging front door of the saloon with the food.

"What are you doing to my floor?!" Joe exclaimed.

Dev quickly left the floor work and met Joe at the front door.

"Give me the food, bartender, and then go on and get out of here. If things work out, we might just buy you a brand-new floor, so make no never mind about what we're doing in here," Dev said as Joe relinquished the two plates of food.

Dev and John stopped long enough to chow down the food that Joe had brought to them and then went back to work on the floorboards. Two or three more boards came off and then, a discovery—one gold coin, lying there on top of the dirt. Just one gold coin.

"What do you make of it, Dev?" John asked. "Did it fall down through one of the cracks or what?"

"Ain't nobody in this town ever had a gold piece like that," Dev said, sneering, "much less let it drop down a crack in the floor without getting it back. Nope, that gold coin was part of the Chacon gold. Somebody has been here and got it all, except for this one gold coin that probably dropped out of a sack. Look at the nails in the last plank we removed, they look brand new, like they have just been nailed in. Now who could've done that to us, John?"

Dev and John were just stating at each other when they came to the same conclusion.

"Joe!" they both said at the same time.

Dev heard a noise outside which broke their eureka moment.

"Looks like a committee of the fine citizens is forming across the street," Dev said, looking at the group of people huddling up. "And looky there, Bird Dog got himself a brand-new hat with no bullet holes in it."

"Hey you! Bird Doo or whatever your name is, come here," Dev hollered.

Even across the street, Dev saw that Bird Dog was fidgeting and looking for a way to hide.

"Come on over here, Bird Doo, I ain't going to shoot you," Dev said loudly. Bird Dog didn't come running; in fact, if a couple people would move out of his way, it looked like Bird Dog would take off running the other way.

Dev sighed, "Oh well," he muttered to himself as he took aim. Bang! Dev shot Bird Dog's hat off again.

"Over here! Now!" Dev yelled at him. "Or the next shot is a bit lower."

Sheepishly, Bird Dog ambled across the street to Dev.

"The bartender, Joe, I want you to get him over here to talk to us," Dev said to Bird Dog.

"Joe? Joe is gone. He loaded up a buggy with a bunch of stuff and took off. He told us that you were tearing up his saloon and there wasn't any need to stay here anymore. Guess you must've scared him pretty good," Bird Dog said, smiling, trying to be friendly with Dev.

Unamused, Dev said, "Quit your bootlicking and go get John's horse and a pack mule with packs. Put some bacon and Arbuckle coffee in the bags. Get John's bedroll and a coffee pot from the store. We will be leaving town, getting out of your hair."

"Don't worry, we're going to pay you for the mule and stuff," Dev said when Bird Dog hesitated. Bird Dog left pretty quick then.

"You better come back with everything pretty soon or I'll come looking for you!" yelled Dev after Bird Dog.

Well, sure as the world, Bird Dog didn't take no time all when he came back, leading John's horse and a pack mule with everything hastily loaded.

John and Dev came out of the saloon. John mounted his horse, with the pack mule tied behind, and took the reins from Bird Dog, turned to leave, and was halted by the sound of one of Dev's guns cocking.

"Hold on right there, Bird Doo," Dev said. "If we don't get out of town safe then you won't either. Walk right along with us till we're out of town." So, the trio went walking through town, right in the middle of the street. Dev had Bird Dog leading the way.

John saw townspeople gathered in little groups here and there, gawking and pointing at them. And there, there was Sally. When John's and Sally's eyes met, Sally just shook her head in disgust. John looked at her as long as he could, then turned forward with his eyes cast downward, knowing that part of his life was gone forever.

"Ok, Bird Doo, you can go back to town now," Dev said when they got out of town. "Just one thing though, where was Joe headed? And you better steer us the right way because you want us to find him. You sure don't want us coming back here empty-handed."

"He said he was headed to Pine," Bird Dog said, stammering. "He said that he knew a feller there by the name of John Hicks, that's all I know."

"All right then," Dev said, looking at Bird Dog very hard, "get on out of here."

Bird Dog took off running back to town. John was watching Big Dog hightailing it when he was startled by Dev's gun firing—*KA BLAM!* Bird Dog's hat flew off of his head again.

"Going to get kind of expensive buying all those new hats, ain't it, Bird Doo?" Dev said dryly.

Bird Dog stopped running, picked up his hat, looked at the neat hole in the crown of it, stuck his finger through the hole, and mumbled to himself as Dev and John left, "And I was at a dead run."

"We'll never catch Joe before he gets to Pine," John said to Dev once they were alone.

"We'll catch him before or after he gets to Pine," Dev said assuredly. "He's in a buggy, remember, the road to Pine isn't much of a road, more trail than road, and rougher than a corn cob where it starts going up."

The day was mostly gone when Dev and John got on Joe's trail real good. Even being on a horse, John found it to be a little difficult keeping up with Dev.

When it got dark, John wanted to stop for the night; Dev didn't. Finally, though, Dev agreed to stop, fearing John's horse would stumble and break a leg on the rough trail that was getting even steeper.

"Well, look here what old Bird Doo packed us," Dev said as he dug out a slab of bacon and a can of peaches. "Maybe I judged that feller all wrong."

John cut off some of the bacon and just impaled it on a stick over the fire to cook. He opened the can of peaches and offered Dev some. Dev turned up his nose at it and instead took a piece of the bacon that didn't appear to be all the way cooked yet.

"Still just meat, Dev," John said, "no vegetables, no fruit ever?"

"Oh yeah, "Dev said, "here it is, my fruit, my vegetables and my grain, all right here in this bottle." Dev displayed a bottle of whiskey that he held up high above his head.

Morning came before John could even see well as he was awakened by Dev shoving a bottle of whiskey in his face.

"Here, have a drink for breakfast and let's get going," Dev said.

"Dab bless it, Dev," John said, moaning. "I've got to take a few minutes to wake up; have some coffee, maybe some breakfast, relieve myself, you know—be a human."

As soon as he said it, he wished that he had not. He saw Dev's eyes flash at him and he saw the old hurt in them.

"Do you think that I am human, John?" Dev said lowly.

"Yes, Dev, you're human," John said apologetically. "You're my brother. You'll always be my brother."

"Okay, John, bust out the coffee pot and the Arbuckle and we'll be human," Dev said, with his eyes still cast downward.

So, they sat there and cooked breakfast and coffee. It was the best breakfast that John could remember having in a long time. It seemed to John that Dev enjoyed it also. He never saw Dev smile and even laugh like that ever. The thought entered John's mind that it could be the ever-present whiskey working on them, or perhaps they were simply being human. "Up and at it," Dev finally announced after breakfast. "Today is the day that we become rich!"

They quickly loaded the packs on the mule, saddled up the horse, and were on their way tracking Joe's buggy tracks up the rough trail.

It didn't take long to come upon the broken-down buggy in the middle of the trail—wheel broken and much of Joe's belongings still lying about.

"Do you see the gold, Dev?" John said, excitedly.

"Nope," Dev said. "The gold, the horse, and Joe are all gone. He didn't even take his food or bedroll. He must be close to where he is going."

Dev and John quickened their pace. John informed Dev that the buggy horse was older and wasn't real good for riding, especially bareback with an unknown amount of gold on its back.

They were close to Pine when they came upon Joe. He looked beat up and barely alive, lying there on the trail.

"Where is it, Joe! Where's the gold!" Dev said menacingly, seeing no gold and no horse.

"Met up with a friend of mine by the name of Hicks," Joe said, gasping. "Him and me were going to take the gold to Mexico but we needed a saddle horse and a pack mule for the gold. My buggy horse went lame carrying me and that gold. Hicks told me that I could get the horse and pack mule not far up the trail at a big house, a ranch, ran by an outfit called 'The Bunch.' I took a bar of gold to pay them. Hicks told me to ask for the owner, someone called 'Old Man.' He said he would go with me except that he had just got fired and ran off from there."

"Where's the gold, Joe?' Dev said again impatiently.

"We stashed the gold bars and the keg of gold coins along the trail," Joe continued. "Hicks said that he would stay near it until I got back with the horse and pack mule, told me that I could walk there easy. It wasn't easy; it was at least two miles straight up until it leveled off into a huge meadow where the house was. Hicks said that they would recognize his horse, so I walked. When I got there though, The Bunch took the bar of gold and locked me up in a cellar, said they were going to hold me for the county sheriff. I've been running from that place. I haven't seen Hicks nor the rest of the gold; he was supposed to be right here—he's gone."

"The Bunch, who is The Bunch?" John chimed in.

"A family and a bunch of hands at a ranch run by someone called 'Old Man.' When I escaped from the cellar, I saw the bar of gold on the kitchen table through the window and I snuck in and got it, but that was a mistake—the dog heard me and started barking. I fought with one of the hands. I grabbed the bar and I ran until I got here and—"

KA POW!

His story was ended by a rifle shot that hit him square in the back. Joe died right there while talking to us.

There were three of them. They came sauntering down the trail. Dev was shocked that he didn't detect their presence. Now the three had the drop on John and Dev.

"Know that feller?" the bearded one asked Dev and John.

John started to answer, but Dev interrupted him quickly.

"Nope. Never seen him before. Who is he? What did he do?" Dev said to them.

"He took something that doesn't belong to him," the bearded one said. "We aim to get it back. Now you, the weird looking one, drop those guns on the ground. And you, stupid looking one, you don't move, hear me?"

"Yeah, we hear you. Don't worry, we don't want any trouble, no trouble at all," Dev said as he slowly just put two hairy fingers on each gun handle.

It was fast, fast as a lightning strike. The three men already had their guns drawn—the bearded one with a rifle already cocked—and it did them no good. They all lay dead, each with an expertly placed bullet hole between their eyes.

John was shaken but looked at each one to make sure they were all dead.

"My God, you shot every one of them right between the eyes!" John said, amazed.

"Body-shot people are people who shoot back before they die," Dev said.

"Gut-shot people take three days to die a horrible death. When you shoot them between the eyes, they don't pull no triggers and they don't suffer much either. If you care about that sort of thing."

"We have to bury them," John said.

"No time, this is the way they're going to get buried." Dev pushed each of them over the side of the trail into a deep, deep canyon.

"Joe too?" John asked.

"Joe too," said Dev as he pushed Joe's body into the canyon.

John was still looking over the edge of the trail, down into the canyon, trying to see Joe's body when Dev interrupted his thoughts.

"That gold is up there at that ranch, John, let's go get it."

"Hold on, Dev," John said, "this fellow Hicks has the gold now, according to what Joe said. Which way do we go? I figure he has it but where did he go? He didn't pass us going down the trail."

"John, that gold has got to be up there with The Bunch by now. Like you said, he didn't pass us on the trail and that ranch is the only place in miles. That Hicks fellow had to go there, right after Joe did."

John mounted his horse, still leading the pack mule. He and Dev had only gone two or three miles when they came upon a three-story ranch house—it was huge.

Dev and John tied up the horse and mule early and made no noise approaching the house on foot. Somehow, though, the house knew that they were there.

"What do you want here!" came a booming voice from the house.

"Must have seen us in the moonlight," Dev whispered to John.

"You know what we want!" Dev hollered back. "That gold is stolen—not yours. If you and that feller named Hicks don't bring it out to us pronto, then we're going to start shooting."

"Ain't nobody named Hicks here!" came the booming voice from inside the house. "Ain't no gold neither. There was a bar of gold brought here by a scoundrel by the name of Joe. We were holding him for the sheriff, but he got away and took the gold with him. Sent three men after him to bring him back, but they haven't come back yet."

"You have the gold!" Dev yelled. "We weren't born yesterday!"

"Don't know what kind of game you lowlives are playing but we don't have any gold," came the answer from the house. "But what we do have is bullets!"

Then came such a volley of bullets from the house that it made a body wonder how there could be that many people with guns in there.

Suddenly, half a dozen men came running out from the left side of the house and six more came from the right side, meaning to flank Dev and John.

"They mean to kill us!" Dev yelled.

"Shoot them, Dev! Shoot!" John exclaimed, his voice breaking.

"There's too many of them, John. There's a time to run, and that's now."

Dev and John ran toward a nearby rocky hill. They were almost there when John caught a bullet in his arm. Dev went back to help John. Bullets were flying everywhere around them.

"Dev," John whined, "go on without me. I can't run. Go on, Dev!"

"I'll come back for you, John. If they kill you, I'll kill all of that scum. I'll come back for you, brother."

Dev ran up the rocky hill but didn't manage to get far. To climb up farther would expose himself to certain death.

He found some rocks to take shelter behind and he returned a few shots with good accuracy. *Curse that moon*, Dev thought to himself as he caught some rock flakes from a ricochet, in his eyes. The moon was so bright that the rocks were actually casting shadows, Dev hunkered down lower to avoid ricochets.

Meanwhile, two men from the ranch came upon John there in the grass, bleeding and becoming faint.

"Kill him!" one said to the other. As they took aim, John managed to speak, "The gold, I know where it is," John lied.

This stopped the men from shooting. "Stop his bleeding. Let's take him to Old Man; he'll know what to do."

They wrapped his arm and frog-walked him to a place behind the ranch house where a cluster of men gathered around a grizzled old cowboy called Old Man.

Old Man hardly even glanced at John. He was ranting about something and pacing back and forth.

John was close enough to hear and make sense of what the Old Man was fretting about. It was the Old Man's granddaughter who had run out of the house, when all the ruckus started, and had somehow fallen down a rock crevice and into a deep hole where none of the men could rescue her. They could hear her crying way down, but they could not see her with their lanterns, nor could they descend into that tight place in order to get her.

"What in the blazes is that blasted hole doing there anyway?" Old Man lamented. "You idiots should have sealed it off. Anything could have fallen in there. You're all hired to protect my animals, my land... and my granddaughter."

Suddenly, Old Man noticed John. John was slumped down on his knees, holding his bleeding arm.

"So, that's one of the lowlives that came to steal what we don't have," Old Man said. "Instead, all they managed to do was to cause my little Heidi, my precious little granddaughter, to run out of the house in the middle of the night and fall down in that blasted hole. No one can even go down in there to help her. God help her! God help me!"

Old Man lifted his downcast head and looked hard at John.

"Hang him! Hang him and let the sun bake him till he rots off of the rope!" Old Man blasted.

The two men that had brought John to Old Man didn't even bother to relay John's story about knowing where the gold was. They lifted him up to take him to a hanging rope, John assumed.

"Dev can help you!" John said loudly. "He could go down there; he could save her. He's probably the only one in the world that could make it down there."

"Wait!" Old Man said. "What did he say? Bring him over here."

The two men quit dragging John away and did an about face and brought him in front of Old Man.

"What did you just say?" Old Man asked John directly.

"I said, Dev—my brother—up there in the rocks, the one that your men have pinned down, aiming to kill him, he could save your granddaughter. He might be the only one alive that could save her."

"What makes you so sure that he could save her? My men tell me and I can see for myself that there ain't no way a human can get down in that godforsaken hole to reach her." "Well, that's just it, sir," John said to Old Man earnestly. "Dev ain't what anyone would call a normal human being. He's on the small side and he's light-ning quick and agile. By his looks, hair being all over his body, some people think that he is half animal. He ran on all fours when he was younger, probably still could if he wanted to. He caught rabbits like a coyote and ate them raw, but he's my brother and he has a good heart. He would help you if you asked him to. We weren't here to rob you. We were after gold that was already stolen and then made off with by Joe, who had no rightful claim to that gold himself."

"That fellow Joe didn't have but one bar of gold on him when we got here," Old Man told John. "He wanted to buy a good horse and a pack mule. It stands to reason that he had intentions to haul a lot more than one bar of gold. I figured he was no good so we were holding him for the law. He weaseled out of the root cellar somehow, snuck into the house, retrieved the bar of gold, and was gone the way he had come. I sent three men after him; what happened to them?"

There was a few seconds of awkward silence because John did not know how to answer. "Well, no matter now," Old Man continued. "The most important thing in the world to me is my granddaughter... down in that hole. You say that the hairy, little feller up there in the rocks that my men are shooting at can save her. Well, I'm here to tell you that I'm sure as Hades willing to let him try if he's willing."

"Jake!" Old Man hollered at one of his hands. "Bandage this one here up proper and make sure that bullet went plum through. After that, get him up to where I'll be, within earshot of that hairy one."

"Rosco!" Old Man yelled even louder at another one. "You get your butt over there and tell the men to stop firing at the one on the hill."

"Yes, sir," Rosco said back. "But I have to tell you, Boss, that one on the hill is a powerful good shot. He's already badly wounded two of the men and all he has up there is a six-shooter."

"Do it! Dag blame it!" was the only answer from Old Man.

All was quiet when John got to where Old Man had taken cover close enough to where Dev could hear them.

"What's your name, boy?" Old Man asked John.

"John, John Durst is my name, sir."

"Ok, John, this is what is going to happen: I'm going to ask him to try to save my granddaughter. If he does, fine, you and he will have my family's eternal gratitude, and any help that I can give to you. But I ain't got no gold. We can try to find this Joe fella for you, find him and maybe find the gold."

"Joe's dead," John blurted out. "Your three men are dead too!"

Old Man put his face down into one large calloused hand. "We'll have to figure that out later," Old Man said. "Right now, I have a little girl to help. When I talk to your brother, I want you to put in your two cents' worth to him and I don't have a lot of time to waste. I have a granddaughter that at least needs to hear my voice over there, got it?"

"I got it," John replied.

"You, you up there on the hill!" Old Man hollered.

"I hear you," Dev said loudly.

"They call me Old Man. I'm the boss here. I've got a proposition for you. My granddaughter is trapped down in a deep hole in the rocks. Nobody here can get to her. The hole is too narrow and my men are too big. Now John here says that you can do the job. If you save her, I'll give you anything you want. I have cattle, horses, land, some money. What do you say?"

"Are you there, John?" Dev asked after a very quiet minute.

"I'm here, Dev."

"Is this on the level?" Dev asked John.

"As far as I know, it is," John answered.

"I want the gold," came Dev's reply.

"Ain't no blasted gold!" Old Man yelled up at Dev. "That man, Joe, had one bar of gold; him and that bar of gold are gone—dead, I hear. I'm getting tired of this and I have a little granddaughter to help. Are you helping us? Or are you staying up there to get shot? What's your answer?"

"Tell your men to hold their fire," said Dev, being a rational sort of man. "I'm coming down to help."

"Hold your fire," Old Man said loudly as he stood up, watching Dev come down the hill.

As Dev got closer, Old Man gasped a little. "Say, you weren't lying about that feller," he said to John. "He's a weird-looking sort. What is he, half coyote?"

"Nope, just hairy," John said, matter-of-factly.

It was getting daylight as Old Man led Dev and John to where the little girl was trapped.

"She's down there," Old Man said, pointing down into a deep, narrow crevice that turned into a hole.

His men had a lantern tied to a rope and lowered it down to try to see, but it only lit up the first twenty feet or so.

"Get more rope, a lot of it," Dev said calmly.

Old Man made a motion with his head and men went scrambling for the rope.

Once they had a pile of rope, Dev instructed them to tie them end to end.

"Tie the rope around my ankles," Dev said to a couple of men.

They moved to do so, but they hesitated when they saw Dev's feet after he had taken his boots off. There was quite a lot of hair and Dev's feet and toes looked a bit weird.

"Give me that blasted rope!" Old Man said, disgusted with his men. "What do you think he is, a coyote or something? He's hairy, that's all!"

John hid his smile with his hand. "Make sure it doesn't come loose," Dev said.

"Ain't coming loose," Old Man grunted as he tied the last knot. "Fact is, that rope is going to have to be cut off."

"Lower me down headfirst," Dev instructed. "If it gets slack, then stop. When I holler, pull it up slow."

Just before Dev was lowered into the crevice, a woman came over to him and laid hands on him. She was crying as she said something under her breath, her head bowed as in prayer. This was the mother of the trapped child, John figured.

John watched Dev being lowered down until he disappeared into the darkness. The men kept feeding rope for what seemed like a long time until, at last, the rope went completely slack.

"I don't hear nothing down there," one of the men said.

"SHHHH!" Old Man shushed him.

Everyone stood looking down into the hole for what seemed like an eternity, then finally they heard Dev yell from far below.

They pulled the rope up slowly. They heard Dev yelling a couple of times and they would stop pulling until they heard him yell again.

Finally, they saw Dev's hairy feet come into view. "My God, he's got her!" one of the men yelled.

John looked down into the hole as hard as he could. It was true, Dev had the little girl; he had pulled her all the way up.

When the men got them both to the top, Old Man grabbed the little girl from Dev and hugged her. The girl's mama, Old Man's daughter, was hugging her also. All three were crying. There weren't many dry eyes in the group of people gathered around them.

"Cut them blasted roped off of that man!" Old Man commanded.

Dev lay there on the ground not moving much, not saying anything.

"My God!" someone exclaimed. "He's been all bit up by snakes!"

Dev had been bitten at least a dozen times by rattlesnakes. There was not a mark on the little girl.

"He's starting to swell up," one of the men said.

"Try to suck some of that poison out of him," Old Man said.

No one moved to do so. No one wanted to touch the hairy, little man.

John flopped down beside Dev and started ripping clothes off of him with his one good arm and trying to suck poison from a dozen bites.

When he had done as much as he could, John lay there sobbing beside Dev. Dev's head was near John, and Dev said something to John.

Heidi

"Don't worry, John, I've been bit before. Besides, I bit every one of them back."

"Take him to the house. Put him in my bed," Old Man said.

The men just stood there looking at each other, not wanting to touch Dev.

Old Man kicked one of the men in his butt. "Dad Blame It! Do what I said."

Three of the men grabbed hold of Dev and carried him into the house.

They let John go into the room where they had taken Dev. Dev lay there in the middle of that great, big bed that belonged to Old Man. John sat by his bedside, quietly sobbing. Dev lay without moving. He was all swollen up like a dog that had eaten bad toads.

"Ain't never slept in a bed this nice," Dev said, quite unexpectedly, to John.

"It's a featherbed, a big one," John said.

"They'll probably burn it after they get me out of it," Dev said, his eyes looking around at the bed without moving his head.

Just then, Andrea, the mother of Heidi, the little girl that Dev had saved, came into the room after quietly knocking on the door.

"Heard talking. Is he able to take some soup?" she asked, surprised that Dev was even talking.

John started to say something, but Dev spoke up instead.

"I'm hungry, ma'am, but I can't move my arms or anything to eat. They are so swollen that I'm afraid that the skin would pop if I tried to move them."

"No need for you to move; I'll feed you," Andrea said, pulling up a chair to do so.

John got up at that point and left the room. He shut the door behind him and stood there in the hall, wiping tears from his eyes with his one unbandaged arm before he went downstairs.

Downstairs, Old Man was seated at the kitchen table with a troubled look on his face.

"John, I've seen a lot of snakebites, but I ain't never seen a person with that many of them. I don't know how he did it but there wasn't one bite on my Heidi." John was exhausted and sat there quietly, listening.

"We owe him," Old Man continued, "and you, a lot. We owe more than we can ever pay. And I've got to tell you, I don't see how he can survive what he has gone through. Sometimes a rattlesnake will bite a person and not even inject poison. But the way that he's swelling up, it's pretty clear that every snake down in that hole did its worst."

"I've got to go and sit with him," John said as he got up to go upstairs again.

Old Man grabbed his arm and motioned for him to sit down. "Sit down here with me. Andrea is up there taking care of him as good as any person can. She owes him a lot too. Let her do what she can for him. The best thing that you and I can do is sit here and wait. I'll get us a bottle to keep us company."

John and Old Man sat there drinking and talking. When the morning sun was well on its way up, John woke to find himself in a bed. He opened the bedroom door to find out that he was just off the main room in the house. There was a large fireplace that was roaring hot. A woman busily moved about the room, cleaning with a dust rag.

"Decided to get up, I see," said the woman when she noticed John. "Breakfast is long over but I'll get you some ham and eggs. Go to the kitchen and I'll tell Old Man that you're up."

John did as he was told. Ham and eggs sounded like heaven to him. He was sitting there smelling the wonderful aroma of breakfast cooking when Old Man came in.

"Morning, John," Old Man said, actually smiling. "You were a little tired last night so I found a bed for you."

"Guess I can't quite keep up with you," John said, wondering why Old Man was so chipper.

"I've got good news, John. We got the doctor here this morning while you were sleeping, and it looks like Dev is going to make it."

"He's all right! Can I see him?"

"Nope, the doctor is still with him. When he gets done with him, he's coming down to look at your arm. If your arm is okay, then come on outside and find me—we have work to do."

John looked at Old Man, wondering if he was joking about working. He wasn't.

After the doctor got done with Dev and gave John the okay on his arm, John went outside to find Old Man as instructed, his arm still in a sling.

Old Man came walking toward him, carrying a basket and a rake. "Figured that you could gather eggs with that one good arm of yours. That's Heidi's job, but she's not feeling up to it yet. When you get done with that, see if you can do any raking over in the horse stall."

John took the basket and the rake from him without saying anything; however, he was thinking plenty. John was no stranger to a chicken coop but wondered how, in the world, he was going to rake.

John managed to gather the eggs with one arm, but when it came to raking, he found it difficult until he took his injured arm out of the sling and used it to brace the rake with.

"Good job, John," said Old Man as he came into the horse stall. "I don't expect that you can shovel and wheelbarrow yet, so just leave it piled up there for a day or two until you can."

This sounded odd to John. Was he a ranch hand now or just working for his keep until Dev was better? It didn't really matter to John though. The work was refreshing and welcome. He ate good here, and the more he worked, the better his arm felt.

About a week after Dev got all snake bit-up, John was sitting on the fence at the round pen, watching the hands work a rough string. Some of the horses were very green. One in particular could not be rode by anyone. Old Man was there and he called for his top hand, Henry, to give it a try.

"If anyone can ride him, Henry can," announced Old Man.

Henry sure tried it, but he too went flying off to land in the soft sand.

"That horse can't be ridden," Henry said as he made his way to the fence, where John and Old Man were.

"Doesn't look unrideable to me," came a voice from behind them.

"Good God, it's Dev!" John said, astonished.

"Think you can do better?" Henry said with a sneer.

"I pretty much know I can," came the reply.

Old Man looked at Dev incredulously. "Are you sure that you want to ride that outlaw? You're fresh out of a sickbed. Why, this is the first time I've seen you out of that room."

"But, Dev, you don't even ride horses," John said.

"Never said that I couldn't ride them," Dev said. "Fact is, they don't like the look of me, think I'm an animal or something."

Old Man hollered, "Catch that horse up for Dev!"

"Cover the eyes so it can't see me getting on!" Dev yelled.

Henry, the top hand, helped catch up and hold the horse for Dev. He doubted Dev's ability to ride that beast, but he respected the courage of the little, hairy man.

Dev said, "Hold my guns for me, John."

Dev strode over to the horse quietly. He got up on the saddle slow and easy, then, with a nod of his head, they let the bronc go.

It was a sight to see. Dev hung onto the bronc like stink on an outhouse. He even kept one hand in the air, showboat style.

Old Man and half the hands were on the fence with their mouths open, watching the show, amazed.

Dev rode that bronc to a standstill, then he quickly dismounted and got away before the horse got a good look at him.

"Guess I am still feeling a little poorly," Dev said to Old Man. "I almost got bucked off!"

Old Man was still open mouthed as he watched Dev start walking back to the house. "Hold on!" he said. "You and John come talk to me in the barn for a minute."

Old Man led them into the barn where it was private. "Boys, I've got no sons, no grandsons, not even a son-in-law, to take over this ranch for me when I can't cut the mustard anymore. I'm offering you enough land for a horse ranch in a beautiful valley eight miles from here. In return, you'll run things at the ranch here, earning money and found until you can build your own house on your own land. The ranch here will be Andrea's and Heidi's."

Old Man let that sink in for a minute, then continued, "Well, there it is, boys, plain and simple. What do you say?"

John and Dev looked at each other with eyes WIDE and mouths open, astonished at the offer.

Old Man said, "Before you answer, I have something that you two need to do for me. It will take care of something that I've been fretting about, and it will give you both time to make sure of your answer to me."

Old Man paused, took his hat off, and looked down at it in his hands.

"We'll do it!" John blurted out awkwardly.

"Hear me out first, boys. I want you to go and bury my three men back there where they lie at the bottom of that canyon just off the trail. I figure that you know where they are. My men say that it ain't going to be an easy task. They could barely spot them down there."

Dev and John agreed to this, and the next morning found them on their way to where they had dumped the men off the trail, into the canyon.

They took with them a quantity of rope and two shovels. It felt good to be on the trail together again. John took his bedroll and one for Dev, thinking that they might spend the night. He even brought some bacon for old times' sake.

They got there before very long at all. They tied the rope around John and Dev wrapped it around a rock and let John down the slope slowly. Dev then tied the rope off and came down very nimbly.

Once they were down where the bodies had come to rest, John wanted to hurry up and get the remains buried. It smelled worse than anything John had ever encountered.

"Ain't nothing that smells worse than a dead, rotting human," Dev said, knowingly.

They buried the three ranch men and placed no crosses on their graves as per the instructions from Old Man. Then they turned their attention to what remained of Joe.

"Your turn," Dev said.

John grimaced and grabbed the shovel to scoop out a grave right next to the remains. Quickly he worked, trying not to look at the rotting, maggot-infested flesh. He had to stop and gag a couple of times. Using the shovel, John dragged the body into the hole as he looked skyward to avoid seeing the hundreds of maggots fall off the rotting flesh.

"Help me throw dirt on him, Dev. The quicker that we get it done, the faster we can get out of here."

Dev grabbed the other shovel and walked over to help as John was slinging dirt on Joe, still not looking at the corpse.

"Hold it, John! Stop!" Dev said loudly. "What is that!"

John forced himself to look down into the hole. The glint of gold showed through the dirt and maggots.

"Gold!" John squealed. "It's the gold bar—it was in his boot!"

Dev fell to his knees and grabbed up the gold bar, wiping the dirt and maggots off of it. Together they sat there in the dirt, ignoring the stench and the flies, admiring the gold bar.

"Are we rich, Dev?" John asked. "Are we rich now?"

"Well, John, one thing for sure, we're a lot richer than we were a few minutes ago."

"What are we going to do with it, Dev? What are we going to spend it on?"

Dev thought quietly for a few minutes, then looked directly at John. "We ought to spend it on our future. We've been offered jobs, and land, by Old Man. I bet that this bar of gold could build us a house on that land. A house of our own, John."

"A future," John said, thoughtfully.

"Feels good to have a future," said Dev. "Might be even better to have a past, to know where you came from, to know who and what you are."

"Let's get out of this place," John said, breaking the silence that followed Dev's words.

They quickly backfilled the dirt into Joe's grave, piled some rocks on top, and placed a hastily made cross for Joe.

They didn't camp that night like John thought they might. As soon as they got back up to the trail, they headed back to the ranch. They had something to show Old Man.

Back at the ranch, Dev and John caught Old Man near the barn and asked him to talk to them in private.

Old Man said, "No problem, boys, I'll talk to you, but first, did you boys do what I asked you to do?"

"We did the job, sir," said John.

"Then my offer is still on the table. What is your answer to me?"

"We accept your offer," said Dev. "Before we shake hands on it, though, maybe you need to take a look at something that we found in Joe's boot."

Inside the barn, Dev dropped the bar of gold onto the work bench.

Old Man reached out and put his fingers on the gleaming metal. "You found that bar of gold that Joe had!"

"We want to build a house, our house, on the land that you offered us," said John.

Old Man slowly fingered the gold bar. "You boys are putting me in a bad box. This bar of gold doesn't belong to you. Don't you see that? If nothing else, we try to be law-abiding here. Outside people call us 'The Bunch,' but we call ourselves a family, and if you're going to be a part of that family, then you have to embrace our tenets."

Dev didn't expect this answer from Old Man. He moved to grab the bar, but Old Man grabbed it first.

"This is for the law," Old Man sternly said.

Dev was frustrated; he wheeled around and walked outside, straight to the round pen. He climbed up and took a sit-down on the top rail to think.

Henry, the top hand, was inside the round pen, riding a nice-looking buckskin, but there was something weird going on. Henry was wearing animal hides from head to toe.

"What in the dickens are you doing, Mr. Top Hand?" Dev asked, sarcastically.

"Well, now that you caught me, I might as well tell you. I was about done with him anyway. I'm breaking this horse for you, Dev. This is one horse that don't care no more if you look like a critter or not."

"I have as much chance of that horse letting me ride him as a June bug has to swim across a duck pond."

Henry got off the horse and handed the reins to Dev. "Why don't you give him a try, Dev?"

"Well, he hasn't bolted so far," Dev said, jumping down from the top rail and moving toward the horse, thinking that as soon as he touched it, it would bolt. He stuck his foot into the stirrup to mount. Then a strange thing happened—the horse didn't bolt, didn't try to run away. It was a first for Dev.

He rode him around the round pen for a few turns and then reined him over near Henry.

"Why did you do this for me, Henry?"

"Well, I figured that anybody that can uncork a bronc like you can would be an awfully good friend to have."

'Friend.' The word seemed odd to Dev.

"I've got nothing to give you, Henry. I can't even buy you a drink."

"Don't want nothing that money buys, Dev. As for a drink, though, maybe you can come over to the bunkhouse some night and pass the bottle around with me and the men. They would like to yarn an hour or two away with you too."

It was a lot for Dev to take in, people that wanted to be his friends, wanted to be... family.

"I'd like that, Henry. I'd like it a lot, thank you."

Dev saw John and Old Man coming toward him out of the corner of his eye. "Excuse me, Henry, I've got something I need to do."

Dev met them halfway across the paddock. "Seems like we forgot to shake hands on our agreement," he said to Old Man. John's face broke into a wide grin.

Old Man grabbed Dev's hand in a powerful, smothering grip of friendship. "Seems like I'm forgetting something, all right. Forgetting that things have happened on all sides that we need to look past. I guess one more thing won't matter much."

With that, Old Man handed the gold bar to Dev. "This is for your house. You two can use as many of the men that will come and help you, as long as it doesn't affect anyone's regular duties here at the ranch."

More handshakes all around and a pull from the jug and it was settled. Within two weeks the first loads of lumber came down the rim road and work started on the house.

The ranch hands took great delight in helping to build the house. Wrap around porch, two living rooms, two chimneys—a dream come true.

Then one day, word of John Hicks came to the ranch. Seems that he and two men named Corey and Gaines were spotted near Rodgers Lake, not far from Flagstaff. They were wanted by the law for another robbery. When the posse appeared on the opposite side of the lake, the three outlaws were observed throwing stuff into the lake. Gaines later died in a gunfight, and Corey wound up in prison. Hicks disappeared again and was rumored to be in Mexico.

Dev was sullen and withdrawn after the news came. Then one morning he started loading his buckskin for a long trip.

Old Man and John came up to Dev as he was tying his bed-roll on.

Old Man said, "Where are you going, Dev, after the gold?"

"Our house is ready to move into," John said. "Remember talking about our future. Our future is here, Dev, your family is here."

"I remember talking about future, John. I remember talking about our past too. Part of my past is missing. Where did I come from? Who was my mother, my father? The gold can go to blazes. I'm going to find my roots."

Dev swung up into the saddle. "I'm only going to go with both of your blessings."

Old Man took off his hat. "Go with our blessings, Dev."

"I'll be back before the snow flies," Dev yelled as he rode off. There was dampness again on his facial hair. *Must be the morning dew*, he thought to himself. Dev figured that he would go up the rim road trail to Long Valley and then to Flagstaff before he went east to New Mexico. Maybe he would check out Rogers Lake, just out of curiosity, where all that outlaw loot was supposedly thrown into the water and mud.

It felt strange to be back on the trail alone, without John, even though he had spent years on the trail by himself. Nights were lonely and he kept thinking of their ranch house and the comforts that it offered. He had a future there but he felt compelled to at least try to find his past.

It was about halfway to Flagstaff when it happened. Dev was still in his bedroll, sleeping late. He had gotten spoiled at the ranch and enjoyed such occasional allowances.

They quietly snuck up on him while he slept. There were two of them—one of them had a gun to his head before he even opened his eyes. He didn't even hear them sneaking up on him—a far cry from the way he used to be.

"Why, looky here what we got, Scratch," the one with the gun to his head said. "He's a weird-looking little feller."

"What do you two want?" Dev asked.

"I want you to get up out of that bedroll and let Scratch and me get a look at you."

Dev didn't wear long johns—no need to with all that hair. There he stood on his bedroll with nary a stich of clothing on.

Scratch came closer, squinting his eyes and his mouth open as he looked at Dev.

"Don't get too close, Scratch! He's a dad-blamed freak or something; he might jump at you."

Scratch jumped back from Dev. He was shaking like a leaf as he held one of Dev's own guns on him.

"We going to shoot him, Clem? I ain't never shot nobody in my whole life. I don't think we should."

"Nope, we ain't going to shoot him; just take everything he's got and leave him out here to be with the other critters."

They both thought that this was a very fine, very funny idea, and so they took everything and rode off laughing, leaving Dev standing there naked.

Now what? Dev thought to himself as he stood there naked. Dev figured that he had to do something. It had to be something that the old Dev would do, not the spoiled Dev that rode a horse, ate breakfast and supper every day, had a drink after work, and slept in late. He had to think like the old Dev, not new Dev.

They were headed toward Flagstaff. Dev had to travel faster than they did and get ahead or at least catch up to them, and he had to do it naked—no clothes, no boots, no guns, no horse.

He followed them as fast as he could, picking his way. The rocks, twigs, and stickers hurt his feet. He was used to wearing boots—his feet were soft. He remembered running on all fours; he couldn't imagine doing that now. It would destroy his hands and feet to do so. Still, he had to move quickly if he had any chance at all to catch up to them. So, he disregarded the pain and started jogging as fast as he could, his feet bleeding, but he did not stop.

It was getting dark when Dev finally caught up to them. He could smell smoke from their fire when he stopped to wait until they went to sleep. Dev's feet hurt and they were bleeding, but there was little he could do about it except to try not to think about it.

When morning came, Dev was fully dressed, his guns strapped on, feet doctored as best he could, socks and boots back on. He built the fire up and was sitting there drinking a cup of coffee when the pair finally woke up.

Clem was first to open his sleepy eyes and see Dev sitting there, looking at him.

"Scratch, we got trouble," Clem said rather calmly.

Scratch rubbed his eyes and looked in disbelief at Dev.

"How did he get here?" he asked stupidly.

"He's here, Scratch, and he's got his guns. Don't know how he did it but he did it."

Dev said, "OK, you two, get them clothes off. We'll see how you do running around out here naked."

With his buckskin horse back under him and leading the two horses of Clem and Scratch with all their gear, Dev took a look back at the near-naked Clem and Scratch, looking very uncomfortable standing there in their long johns watching Dev leave.

Dev, feeling very good about himself, kept going until he knew that the pair could not possibly catch up before he stopped to camp at Lake Carleton, which was a dry lake, most of the time, south of Flagstaff. It was cold at camp that night, but Dev had a big blazing fire—not the same sort of fire that he would have had back in his bounty hunter days. Then he started thinking about the two men that he left, in their underwear, back on the trail. He must be getting soft, he thought to himself. Fact is, he felt sorry for them.

Dev couldn't believe it, but the next morning he found himself riding back to the hapless pair with their horses and clothes in tow. It was apparent that they didn't get much sleep during the cold night because when Dev found them, they were on the ground covered in sticks and twigs and looked like two gophers coming out of their hole.

"You two boys look pretty comfortable. Maybe I should come back tomorrow."

Clem and Scratch jumped up awkwardly, shaking the vegetation from their head and face.

"Please don't go! We're freezing to death out here. We'll do anything that you ask. Please help us."

Dev looked at the pair, studying them. "OK, boys, I'll help you this time, but if you cross me again, it will go bad for you, very bad."

The two fell to their knees, crying. "Thank you, thank you," they blubbered.

"Get up off of your knees and come and get your clothes. You can have your guns but no bullets until you prove yourselves."

"Yes, sir. Yes, sir. Thank you. Thank you," they whined as they put their clothes on, shakily.

Once the pair had dressed and regained a little of their composure, Dev had them mount up and they all headed to Dev's previous camp near Lake Carleton. Dev had them kill a couple of rattlesnakes on the way there. They did this willingly but asked Dev why he wanted them.

Dev said, "We'll gather a few things on the way to camp. When we get there, I'll fix you boys a big pot of 'Son of a Gun' stew. That's something that Old Man taught me how to make."

Clem and Scratch had no idea what or whom Dev was talking about. But with the prospect of getting fed, they eagerly did what they were told to do—picking this root and those leaves and the snakes which they eyeballed warily, never even hearing of people eating them.

True to his word, when they got to the dry lake camp, Dev prepared the snakes, chopped up this and that, got a big pot of water on the fire, and started cooking supper. After a while and a good dose of salt and a fresh pot of coffee, they all had a meal as good as any of them could recall.

Dev didn't fully understand why he showed such mercy to the pair. Back in his bounty hunter days, he would have probably killed them both. Now, it seemed that he needed human companionship. Yes, he had changed. Was it a good thing? He did not know, but it was sure a fact.

The next morning, Dev got the boys up early. Wanting to know if they were still in a state of mind to take orders, Dev had them set up targets for him to shoot. Then he even had them hold various things out for him to shoot from their hands. Far from being reluctant or argumentative about it, they were thrilled to do it, even when he had Clem put a pine cone on top of Scratch's head at 20 paces. They both laughed with absolute joy when Dev shot it off. Dev reckoned that he wasn't dealing with geniuses.

Fun and breakfast over, they headed on into Flagstaff and picked up supplies and a couple of shovels.

"Where are you going? Rogers Lake?" asked the storekeeper.

"Yep," Dev said simply.

"That place has more holes dug in it than a prairie dog town and nobody found nothing," said a loafer that was hanging around the store, apparently content to stare at Dev.

"Maybe they're digging in the wrong place," Dev said as he turned to leave, not wanting to talk more.

Dev knew that Hicks was a sneaky type, and smart. Stands to reason that the gold ain't where everybody was led to believe it was.

With fresh supplies and shovels, Dev and the duo headed out to Rogers Lake, a half day's ride away. It wasn't hard figuring out where everybody thought the loot was. There were holes dug into the not quite dried up Rogers Lake bed everywhere.

"Well, this is where they think the loot was thrown in," Dev said." Obviously, it ain't here and probably never was."

"But this is where the posse saw them throw it in," Clem said.

"They were plumb on the other side of the lake when they saw them throw something in. Then they had to ride all the way around before they even started to try and track them. I figure that the loot isn't in the lake mud and never was. Oh, it's buried, all right, but where? That's what we have to figure out, boys. Let's see if we can find where the outlaws camped. That's probably where the loot is buried. That's not going to be easy though because half the town's people have been out here camping, drinking, and digging."

Sure enough, it was impossible. It looked like a thousand people had camped out in the woods near the lake. Where the outlaws had camped was probably covered by townspeople trampings.

Dev sat down on a stump to think. "If I was an outlaw, or maybe even if I wasn't, I would camp where my campfire wasn't so visible at night. A place like up that drainage there, behind that mound of dirt," he said as he stood up and pointed.

Clem and Scratch jumped up in unison and started running toward the dry wash. Dev just sat there watching them as they disappeared up the wash and behind the mound of dirt. Clem appeared back on top of the dirt mound.

"There was a camp here, sure enough!" he yelled.

Dev got up and slowly walked toward the wash. Clem and Scratch passed him in a blur as they ran back to get shovels. When Dev got there, he stood on the dirt mound and surveyed the camp carefully.

There it was—right in the middle of the dry cow pond behind the mound—disturbed dirt! That had to be the place.

By then, the boys were back with their shovels and they started frantically digging and slinging dirt everywhere. Dev slowly walked down the slope and stood right where he figured the loot was buried.

"Dig right here!" he announced loudly. Clem and Scratch were on it like ravens on buffalo chips, digging as fast as they could.

"It's here!" Clem yelled, falling to his knees and trying to pull a bar of gold out of the dirt. He was grunting as he switched from trying to pull the bar out and digging like a dog with his hands.

"Calm down, boys, that bar is longer than you think, and heavier too. It's going to take some doing to dig it, and whatever else is in that hole, out. Take turns digging around the area and then work in. But calm down, it's going to take a while."

And it did take a while. When it was done, the boys had dug up eight gold bars—each one was three feet long and four inches wide, weighing seventy pounds. In addition, there were eleven smaller bars of gold similar to the one that Dev and John had found in Joe's boot and a small wooden keg full of double eagles.

"How does it feel to be rich?" Dev asked Clem and Scratch.

"It feels weird," Scratch said. "I ain't never had more than a few dollars at a time ever in my life."

"Can we drink that bottle of whiskey tonight, sorta like a celebration?" Clem blurted out.

"We can drink that whole dang bottle and more if we had it cause… we're rich!" Scratch gushed.

That night, Dev kept thinking about things that Old Man had said. About doing right by the law, living under the tenets of the family, and having honor.

Next morning, Dev told Clem and Scratch to go into town and buy a rig with a team with which to haul the loot. He would have gone himself but he wanted to keep an eye on the loot. One of the three outlaws was dead and another was in prison. But Hicks was still at large somewhere and it made sense that he might come back for the loot.

"Don't you two tell anybody what we found," Dev told Clem and Scratch. "Just take what money I have left in my pocket and get a rig and one bottle of whiskey to celebrate."

"We ain't gonna tell nobody," said Clem.

"Nobody," repeated Scratch.

Dev had time for a long, hard think while the boys were gone. When he finally heard them coming back, he knew what he must do.

They loaded up the wagon and headed for Flagstaff. Dev wanted to explain what was on his mind to do, but he just couldn't bring himself to say the words. He had the boys drive the wagon right into town and straight to the sheriff's office. Clem and Scratch blindly did what Dev told them to do, thinking that he had their best interest at heart. But when they got to the sheriff's office, a crowd of people started gathering around, the sheriff came out, and all of a sudden, it was like the Fourth of July around them. People started shouting and hollering and jumping up and down, celebrating. They were saying how Dev and the boys were some kind of heroes and started dragging them toward the saloon to buy them drinks.

Clem looked back at the wagon with the gold as they were being dragged away from it.

"Dev, what about our gold?" he said, bewildered.

"It's not our gold, Clem—it never was. It's up to the law to get it back to whom it belongs to," Dev said in a sad, sorry way.

The townspeople bought them drinks all night long. They even put them up in the hotel next morning. After a few hours' sleep, Dev got up and started looking for the boys. He found them on the back porch of the hotel, quietly talking to each other.

"What's going on, boys?" Dev asked.

"You said that we were going to be rich," Scratch said, almost crying.

"You lied to us," Clem said accusingly.

Dev said, "Everything that you are saying is true. I did lie to you, but that night at camp, I got to thinking about things that somebody told me not too long ago. About things in our lives that are more important than gold, things like family, belonging to something, doing right, living by the law—and by God. About having a future with honor."

The boys didn't say much, but Dev got the impression that they didn't appreciate their reversal of fortune. They thought they were going to be rich, and now they were the same two uneducated, unwanted, broke pair of losers that they were before.

Things were beginning to calm down in town. People still bought Dev and the boys drinks and slapped them on their backs, but things were quickly going back to normal. Dev knew it was time to leave when the hotel owner asked him how much longer he planned to stay because the saloon contributions toward their rooms were drying up.

Dev gathered his belongings and tied them to his horse. He had sold the rig that they used to haul the loot. The boys had their own horses and whatever they had before. They were still in town but didn't have much to do with Dev since being denied the riches that they thought they were going to get.

All that was left for Dev to do was leave. Where to go? *New Mexico*, Dev reckoned, *where it all began.* Back to where Grandpa shot him, where John first saw him—naked and animal like. Hopefully, he would find answers there.

Dev rode east out of town toward New Mexico Territory to find his past. Suddenly he heard horses behind him. It was Clem and Scratch.

"Where are you going, Dev?" asked Clem.

Dev kept on riding. "Thought you two didn't have no use for me anymore."

"We got to thinking about it. Thinking really hard about the things you said. Things like belonging somewhere, being a part of something, about living right and doing right."

Clem rode his horse in front of Dev and turned it sideways, forcing Dev to stop and look at him. "Me and Scratch ain't never belonged nowhere. Nobody ever wanted us, not even our folks. Maybe we are a lot like you. I guess what we're trying to say is, can we stick with you, be part of something, part of a family?"

Dev looked down at his hands and then dismounted on the Indian side, away from Clem and Scratch.

"Darn cinch keeps slipping," Dev said, wiping that annoying wetness from his eyes again.

"The cinch is on the other side," Scratch said, trying to be helpful in his naïve way.

Dev got back up on his horse from the Indian side, muttering to himself, "This blasted civilized life is changing me from bad to something worse."

"What's that? I can't hear you," Clem said.

"I was just saying that a future, a future with family and with honor, is a much better thing than a past. Your past is like campfire smoke, sometimes it chases some people, smothers them, runs them away—that's my past. Sometimes it goes straight up, fast, amounts to nothing, even takes the heat, the comfort with it—that's you boys. That's why the future is what we all should look toward, not the past. Come on, boys, we have a great future to go to."

"Can we cook son-of-a-gun stew again, Dev?" Scratch said excitedly.

"Sure, we can, except no lizards this time, just snake or rabbit."

It took four days of leisurely travel and several pots of son-of-a-gun, but finally they arrived home.

Old Man greeted them all at the main house. "Welcome home, Dev. Did you find your past?"

"Found something better, much better."

Old Man didn't understand Dev's answer, but it didn't matter. He was just glad to see Dev back.

"These are two friends of mine who would like to be part of something," Dev said.

"Well, I know a ranch just starting up about eight miles from here. They have plenty of work for two young fellers to do. Tonight, though, we're going to spin some yarns and pass the bottle. I've been got a big pot of son-of-a-gun stew to eat."

"Ohhhhh," moaned Scratch, holding his belly.

Clem and Scratch turned out to be good workers at Dev and John's ranch. The future looked good for everybody.

Then came word from Flagstaff, in the form of a newspaper, about the recovered loot and the people that had found it and turned it over to the law.

Andrea read the newspaper article to everyone at a special supper one night. John and Old Man were astonished that none of the three of them had said a word about the adventure.

Old Man said, "You boys had all the gold that you could ever want. What made you turn it over to the law?"

"Dev told us about the things that mattered more than gold that he had learned. About doing right, about honor, family, about belonging to something."

The whole group was silent for a minute. Then Old Man spoke, "I'm proud of all of you."

"That's not all of the article," Andrea said. "It goes on to say that only the eight long bars of gold and the keg of double eagles can be accounted for as stolen. There is no record anywhere of the rest of the gold having been stolen. They say that Dev, Clem, and Scratch can lay claim to it legally anytime that they show up to do so."

There was quiet for at least another minute.

"Golly!" said Scratch. "We are rich!"